star struck

Also by Pamela Anderson
STAR

star struck

pamela anderson

ATRIA BOOKS
New York London Toronto Sydney

ATRIA BOOKS
1230 Avenue of the Americas
New York, NY 10020

ISBN 13: 978-0-7434-9283-6
ISBN 10:   0-7434-9283-8

First Atria Books hardcover edition August 2005

10 9 8 7 6 5 4 3 2 1

ATRIA BOOKS is a trademark of Simon & Schuster, Inc.

For information regarding special discounts for bulk purchases,
please contact Simon & Schuster Special Sales at 1-800-456-6798
or business@simonandschuster.com.

Manufactured in the United States of America

To my mom—
the nut doesn't fall far from the tree.

acknowledgments

THANKS

To Mom and Dad for having a sense of humor and supplying me with one in the face of life's ups and downs.

To my brother, Gerry Anderson, for being there for me through thick and thin, and for helping me with this manuscript and supplying great advice and direction/confirmation—huge help! He's such a talent—writer, producer, and director . . . watch out!

To my children, Brando and Dilly, whom I love desperately, for giving me the idea and inspiration for staying home and writing so I could spend more time with them . . . the universe *does* validate good decisions.

To Eric Shaw Quinn—of course . . . my partner in crime on this project—are you me or am I you? The lines have blurred and you are wearing my shoes . . . and they're trashed—you've walked more than a mile!

To my editor, Brenda . . . you have always been a great supporter and believed in this from the start . . . another bestseller to add to your list? Thank you for everything.

To Judith—the boss at Simon and Schuster!—thanks for

allowing me to be creative and not forcing me into a "Pammyland" concept! I'm on to you—all is forgiven.

To Hefner, for helping to build interesting adventures in our lives, empowering women . . . and for just being you!

To David LaChapelle, Luca, and Jesus . . . talented, genius, eccentric, and honest! My favorite people—friends whom I lean on and who put me out if I catch on fire You remind me of what's important besides family: *art*.

To all the people I love and work with . . . and whom make life easier . . . or just more interesting . . . especiailly: everyone at PETA, and Dan Mathews (my other gay husband), everyone at MAC, Melanie Arthur, Lori and Kylie Anderson, Michael Ullman, Barry Tyerman, Steven Pranica, Amanda, Tommy, Chef Jay, Charisse, Sue, Harper and Michael, Jamie, J. P., Steve Levitan, and everyone at *Stacked,* Spade, Stern, Leno . . . and/or whoever I'm . . .

Don't try this at home!

star struck

1

you shook me all
night long

Why do my nipples hurt? was Star's first thought as she woke from a strangely deep sleep, her hands gliding along her naked body to the tender nipples that had awakened her. She winced as she made contact, realizing only belatedly that she was naked. Star tried to open her eyes but couldn't; the room was too bright. She raised her hand to shield her view, only to be blinded by a huge diamond ring that hadn't been on her finger when she went to sleep.

When *had* she gone to sleep? And where?

Stretching, Star reached up to push back her hair as she tried to get her bearings and she struck herself on the forehead with the chrome handle of the Colt .45 she was holding in her right hand. She screamed and fell off the dresser on which she'd been perched. The gun went off, taking out a glass table top that shattered into four-carat chunks of safety glass.

Star stared at the revolver in her hand. She'd never even touched a gun before, but here she was, naked except for a pair of Gucci boots, a strange diamond ring, and a gun welded to her hand.

What the hell was going on?

Why did everything feel so strange? So blurry?

She was hungry but didn't have an appetite. Her skin felt alive, vibrating gently against her every nerve ending. The sun was so bright she could hardly see and the carpet was so soft it tickled her bare ass where she sat, puzzled, on the floor.

Looking around, Star was relieved to see that she was still in her hotel room in Cabo. Well, what was left of her hotel room. Pictures had been torn off the wall and defaced; cushions from the chairs and sofa had been built into a fort in the middle of the room; tables were stacked to the ceiling; and dozens of empty Cristal bottles, scattered everywhere, prompted her to wonder if the damages would be covered under the "incidentals" clause in her modeling contract.

As she further surveyed the damage, Star noticed the un-made bed that was a confusion of sheets, pillows, and strangely chosen items from around the room—a candlestick, an ice bucket, and a selection of well-placed objets d'art. Condoms, some used, some blown up like balloons, also littered the space. "Well, I'm glad we played safe," she said with a lit-tle laugh, swatting one of the oddly shaped balloons out of her way. That's when she saw the tiny video camera and a few dozen tapes strewn across the coffee table, along with the remnants of several lines of cocaine. How odd, Star reflected. I don't do drugs. I wonder who's been here? Her musings turned to panic as she saw a pair of bare feet sticking out from beneath the tangle of Frette sheets, next to a blender that must have been taken from the room's wet bar. Actually, the blender was working double duty because its cord had been used to bind the mysterious pair of ankles to the bedposts.

A modern-day Goldilocks, Star crept closer. Who are these feet attached to? And what are they doing in my bed? Tentatively, she reached out and touched a big toe with the barrel of the gun. A small, strangled cry escaped her throat as the toe responded, wiggling as if to get away from the cold steel barrel. Star put her hand over her mouth, felt the strange diamond against her cheek, and pulled it away.

She felt so naked.

Well, aside from the boots and the ring, she was naked. But it wasn't just that she didn't have any clothes on. She felt vulnerable—raw and exposed. Try as she might, she could not remember what had happened last night, could not remember how she'd wound up asleep on the dresser, and could not guess who this might be in her bed. She stood frozen for a minute, listening to the muffled cries coming from under the sheets.

Star made her way around the bed looking for clues to identify the stranger. She found nothing. It was a man; that much was clear from the rather sizable tent pole raised under the sheets. But who? Surely, she would remember an erection like that, she thought with a playful giggle, reaching out and giving the massive morning wood a tap. The moans changed, a different tone now, at least an octave lower.

Finally, she could stand it no longer. She reached for the hem of the crumpled sheet, ready to expose the identity of the well-endowed stranger . . . but then her phone rang, startling her as it played its version of "You Shook Me All Night Long."

Star pulled back, oddly frightened by the old AC/DC song that had shattered the silence.

Should she answer it?

The phone rang again. It echoed in the room and in her head.

Would it seem suspicious not to answer it?

It rang.

And rang.

What time was it anyway?

Taking a deep breath, Star answered it.

"Hello?" she said softly, moving away from the body in the bed.

"Star? Honey, is that you?"

"Who is this?"

"It's Rufus," the caller said with a startled laugh.

She considered the information for a moment. Everything seemed so strange. She felt dizzy and medicated.

"Your boyfriend?" he said, when she didn't answer, an edge in his voice.

"Hi, baby, I'm sorry," she said, scratching her nose with the gun. "I just woke up and I'm not feeling right."

"Not feeling right?" he said, curious at her strange choice of words. "What do you mean, 'not feeling right'? And *why* are you whispering?"

"Are you working for the CIA?" she asked sharply, closing the bathroom door behind her.

"What?"

"Well, I just thought, what with the third degree you were interrogating me," she snapped.

"I'm sorry," he said gently. "You just seem so strange."

"Well, I *feel* strange," she continued. "Isn't that what I've been trying to tell you?"

"Is everything all right?" he asked, genuinely confused.

"I'll have to get back to you when I know, but thanks for your concern." Star clicked off the phone, regarding it irritably for a moment before dropping it into the toilet.

Her captive was waiting patiently for her when she returned to the bed.

"What did I do last night?" she asked herself.

And then, with a child's impatience on Christmas morning, she tore off the sheet and found herself staring into the face of the rock-and-roll musician Jimi Deed, bound, gagged, and tied to her bed. Star hadn't seen Jimi since she threw him out of her trailer back on the California set of her TV show, *Lifeguards, Inc.* The only way she'd been able to convince him to leave had been to agree to go out with him when she got back from Cabo, though he'd called persistently and threatened to follow her. She was *still* in Cabo, and yet here he was.

"What are you doing here?" she demanded, unconsciously waving the gun at him.

Jimi winced, crying out in fear as the barrel of the shiny pistol passed near his nose.

"Oh, sorry about that," she said, embarrassed and apologetic, although continuing to wave the gun around. "It's not mine," she explained. "I'm not sure how it got here. For that matter, I'm not sure how *you* got here. I'm not really a gun person; I don't even know how it works, really. I mean, I guess you just pull on . . ."

And with that, the room was suddenly and violently filled

with feathers raining down like the first snow of the season. Jimi screamed through his gag and writhed wildly on the bed, his head next to the blackened remains of the pillow she'd shot out from under him. She looked like an angel with a .45.

"Oh . . . I'm so very sorry," she said, putting the gun on the bedside table. "You don't look too dangerous. Well not most of you, anyway," she said, lifting the sheet for a peek under the big tent he was pitching. She gave a low appreciative whistle. "Looks like you've got a bigger pistol than me."

Jimi struggled vainly against his bonds, startling Star. She dropped the sheet, frightened, but soon realized that he was no threat to her in his present condition.

"So how did you wind up here?" she said, sitting down beside him.

Jimi made some rather defiant noises through his gag.

"Oh, right, the gag," she said, knocking herself in the forehead with the heel of her hand. "My bad. Now, no screaming. I doubt anyone would hear you or, judging from this room, care. But I've got a really bad hangover from all this champagne, so, shhh."

Star unbuckled the very professional ballgag that was in his mouth, allowing him to spit out the orange ball.

"What the fuck?" he demanded.

"What do you mean?" Star said, rising. "And what the hell are you doing in my hotel room?"

"I'm tied to the bed and you've got a gun," he said. "Two plus two."

"When did you get here?" she asked, still puzzled. "What happened last night?"

"I've been here for three days," he said. "Last night just made it clear I should have left after two. Or killed you. Now will you let me go? I was supposed to be somewhere last night."

"You've been here with me for three days?" Star asked, not really paying much attention to what he'd said after that. "How is that possible?"

"Are you going to let me go?"

"I don't know. Do you promise not to tell anyone about all this?"

"I promise I'll visit you in Mexican jail," Jimi snarled, straining at his bonds.

"Now you have to promise me that you won't get me in trouble," Star said, rising, alarmed by his belligerent attitude even in his present circumstances.

"Are you fucking kidding me?" he said with a snort of laughter. "You kidnapped me and tied me up at gunpoint."

"Oh that's ridiculous," Star said, laughing. "I've never had to tie a man up, unless he wanted me to."

"Well, it seemed hot at first," Jimi admitted, doing what he could to shrug. "But then you wouldn't let me go, and that's kidnapping."

"You seem pretty glad to see me this morning," she said, reaching out and playfully tweaking the persistent erection, tenting the sheets in front of him. "Maybe we could work something out."

"Work something out?"

"Well, used to be you wanted to date me pretty bad, as I remember."

"That was before I married you and you tied me up and kidnapped me!" he roared. "Now all I want to do is see you behind bars."

"M-m-m-married?" Star stuttered. "I'm married?"

"Since yesterday."

"My mom is definitely not going to approve of this."

"She was pretty pissed," Jimi laughed.

"She was here?"

"No, you called her to tell her," Jimi nodded smugly.

"Oh my God."

"What else happened? How did you get here?"

"You really don't remember, do you?"

Star only shook her head in answer.

"I'll make you a deal," Jimi said. "You untie me and let me go to the bathroom, and I'll tell you what happened."

"No, I don't think I can trust you yet."

"We're married," Jimi said with a touch of self-righteousness.

She looked at him.

"Okay, so that doesn't count for much," he agreed. "But I really do have to pee."

She looked around the room and found the solution—an ice bucket, filled with slush and an upended bottle of Cristal. She arose from the bed where she'd been sitting, grabbed the bucket, and, marching out onto the balcony of her top-floor rooms, dumped the contents down the combined heights of the high-rise hotel and the steep cliffs on which it sat, into the Pacific, hundreds of feet below.

Leaving the French windows open, she walked back to the bed where he lay and pulled back the sheets.

"I can't believe I don't remember this," she said, taking his cock in her hand and guiding it into the ice bucket.

"You can't be serious!" he snarled.

"Roll over as much as you can," Star said playfully. "It's time for a little game of fireman and hose."

"Fuck you."

"Suit yourself," she shrugged, taking the bucket away.

"I'll piss right here," he said defiantly.

"And you'll lie in it," she said, folding her arms under her naked breasts.

"Mother fuck," he said, turning his hips as much toward her as he could, bound to the bed as he was.

"Oh, you want the bucket back now?"

"Just put it over here."

"Say please."

"Please," he said through gritted teeth.

Once again she took his cock in her hand and guided it into the bucket.

"Wow," she observed, looking at the almost-full bucket.

"Well, I've been tied up since last night."

"Okay then . . ." Returning from the bathroom where she'd emptied the bucket, Star took a seat on the bed, legs folded Indian style beside Jimi's naked body. "So, tell me what happened."

"You didn't untie me," he said, turning his head away.

"Tell me," she said, reaching out and toying with his now deflated cock.

"No," he said. "Cut it out."

"Tell me," she coaxed, stroking him back to erection.

He shook his head violently from side to side.

"Come on," she said, stroking harder.

"Get the fuck off of me," he protested.

"If you tell."

"Fuck you."

Laughing, she grabbed some hand cream from the bedside table and slathered it onto her hands and his erection. Mercilessly she began again, stroking and stroking until his balls tightened and he neared the brink. Abruptly she stopped and let him subside. As his orgasm faded she resumed her tease, stroking, sucking, and riding him near to orgasm. Again and again she played, always stopping just before he finished, until he was screaming and begging for release.

"Please, please, now," he pleaded as she rode him once more to the edge.

"Will you tell?" she asked, slowing down and letting him subside again.

"No, fuck you!" he spat.

"Okay, then," she said, climbing off. She spotted the video camera on the coffee table and brought it back with her. "Smile for the camera," she said, straddling him once more. She taped the two of them as best she could from her position astride him. She was driving him slowly mad, and enjoying every minute of it.

"I'll do it, I'll do it, I'll do anything, just don't fucking stop!" he screamed as she brought him to the brink once more.

"How can I believe you?" she asked, turning to film his answer.

"I don't know," he said. "I give you my word."

"I must have tied you up for a reason," she said. "I'm not sure about your word. Tell me something that I can use against you if you go back on your promise. Something nobody else knows."

"I was involved in a hit-and-run accident a couple of years back."

"You're a rock star," she scoffed. "That's like a rite of passage. What else?"

"I used to pay for studio time by screwing the woman who ran the recording studio."

"You've probably been bragging about that one for years," she said dismissively, picking up the pace and riding him harder. "Tell me *real* secrets."

"I used to take tap and ballet classes in high school," he blurted out, desperate. "And I was really good. My mom has recital pictures in her living room."

"That's the stuff," she said, bearing down. She had managed to get herself off a few times in the process, but managed to score one more off of her captive before he lost it and erupted, screaming and writhing in his relief.

She fell to one side and they lay panting next to each other for a bit.

"You raped me," he said.

"Raped you? Me?" she said, rewinding the tape and playing it back for him in the viewfinder.

"Please, please, now," his voice rang out. "Oh fuck yeah."

"Yeah, you sound like a rape victim," she said, giving him a swat. "Now, tell me the story.

The trip to Cabo had seemed like the perfect escape. Between her simultaneous shooting schedules for *Hammer Time* and *Lifeguards, Inc.,* her public appearances to promote both shows, and keeping the investors happy at her nightclub, Ka Mano, while juggling a personal life that included dating both Rufus and Mando, Star was, as she liked to say, "blowing the candle at both ends." In her sparc time, she was also building a reputation as a photographer's model. Star's gatefold debut in *Mann* magazine had provided the bare essentials to start her modeling career. While she had added clothes to her modeling with some success, "less is more" best described her career, much to her mom's chagrin.

The trip to Cabo had come to Star through her friend and mentor, Jayne. A designer-label suntan-lotion company had come to *Mann* for models. And once again, Jayne's position as the magazine's executive editor and Star's dear friend had been a godsend to Star. As usual, Star's manager had arranged things and taken the credit along with his percentage, but it was her old friend who'd not only hooked her up but pushed her to take the assignment.

And so Star headed south of the border, as much for the promise of a vacation as the work.

It was a promise kept. Each day she spent a few hours shooting with a group of other models. She was the centerpiece of the promotion, but the whole shoot didn't rest on her. After hours—aka early afternoon—she was free to while away her time at the fashionable seaside resort, where she had been put up in the top-floor El Presidente suite.

The water was brisk, refreshing, and as blue as she'd ever seen.

The hotel, perched atop steep cliffs above the Pacific, looked as if it had been bleached white in the sun, in sharp contrast to the lush tropical plants and flowers that grew like weeds.

Star's rooms at the Cabo Ritz were party headquarters for the crew and models. It was off-season and the town had turned back into a sleepy fishing village where there was little to do, so they made their own fun.

There was some nightlife, though it was pitched primarily

to the spring-break crowd and the sort of lowlifes who'd want to spend the evening at such dissolute debaucheries, and Star couldn't figure out why no one in the cast or crew seemed interested.

So, when the phone rang during yet another afternoon nap, more than anything she'd actually thought it was going to be the production manager, the only person who'd actually called the room since her arrival.

"Star?"

"Yeah."

"I was hoping it would be you."

"Who were you expecting?"

"You got no idea how many Estrellitas I've talked to in the last twelve hours."

"What?"

"It means 'little star.' "

"Who is this?"

"Let me give you a hint," he said, clearing his throat and singing. "Oh, my penis has a first name, it's L-A-R-G-E—"

She hung up.

The phone rang again.

"Goddamn it!" she screamed into the phone. "How did you get this number? I told you I'd see you when I got back from the shoot—"

"Miss Leigh?" the production manager asked tentatively, interrupting her tirade. "Is everything all right?"

"Oh, Herb, I'm sorry, I . . ." Star trailed off, embarrassed. "I thought you were someone else."

"Jeez, who's been calling your room?"

"Doesn't matter," Star said, laughing it off. "I think he got the message. What's up?"

They had a brief conversation about the schedule for her last day of shooting.

"Okay, I'll see you in the morning," Star said. "Adidas."

"Adios." Herb laughed as he hung up.

The phone rang again almost immediately, and she naturally assumed it was Herb.

"What did you forget?" she answered.

"Are you having a bad day?"

"Am I?" Star said, a warning in her voice. "Maybe I'm just confused, but I was sure we'd agreed that I would go out with you when I got back to L.A. and that you wouldn't bug me before I got back."

"Well, that was before this bad mood," Jimi explained reasonably. "Me and some of the boys just happened to be in Cabo—and not a minute too soon, it sounds like. So, if you'd just tell me your room number, we'll come right on up and get started on cheering you up."

"Here?" Star demanded. "You're here?"

"Well, the call's not coming from inside the house, but—"

She hung up.

Almost immediately, the phone began to ring again.

She stared at it.

She wondered how he could dial that fast.

It kept ringing.

She put it in the drawer of her bedside table.

It rang and rang and rang.

"What?" she said, snatching open the drawer and answering it at last.

"What's your room number. I can be there in—"

"Oh, no," Star said, curious but wary. "How did you find me?"

"Well, you told me you were going to Cabo," Jimi snorted. "And the rest was easy. I just called every hotel until I found you."

"Persistent."

"I think you're worth it."

"You do, hunh?" she said, at last intrigued.

"I'm here, aren't I?"

"Yeah, you are."

"Ninety-nine percent of success is showing up."

"What's the other one percent?" She giggled.

"Truly amazing talent," he said with a rumble of husky laughter.

"Are you talented?"

"You have no idea."

"No, I don't, actually." Star giggled.

And so it began.

It just wasn't possible to tell him no.

After talking with Jimi on the phone for three hours that first day, Star agreed that she and her friends from the shoot would meet him and his friends for drinks at the hotel bar. It seemed like innocent fun, and it was, at long last, something to do on her vacation that involved leaving her room besides work. Star had had just about all the rest and relaxation she could stand, and a little tequila and a lot of dancing sounded like just what her holiday needed.

Best of all, it was the first offer she'd made the others on the shoot that had drawn any interest at all. Missy, her makeup and hair girl, three of the other models—Diane, Cindy, and Kat—and Roberto, one of the boys on the crew

who was also one of the girls, all jumped at the chance to
come along to see what would happen that evening.

Just knowing that they were going out that night enlivened
Star on the next day's shoot. She'd made quite the hit learning
to windsurf for the cameras. Afterward, she'd snagged some
of the summer line they were there to model and enlisted
Missy, who'd been doing her makeup for the shoot, to help
her get ready so she could make a real entrance at the bar that
night. She made quite the project of it.

The truth of it was, Star hadn't been all that interested
in Jimi. She didn't even intend to see him after she got back
to L.A.

"Okay, Missy," Star said, making like she was cracking a
whip as she emerged wearing a bikini top, Gucci short shorts,
and stilettos. "Bring on the eyeliner."

"I'm sorry, but the señor will not be permitted in the hotel
bar," the maître d' said with a little sniff. "You are not dressed
properly for the Ritz. Perhaps the Hilton will be more to
the señor's liking? They have no standards there that I can
detect."

Star, Missy, and the others were enjoying the show from
their table inside the Land's End, the bar to which the maître
d' was attempting to refuse entry to Jimi and his scruffy lot.
Clad more or less identically in saggy jeans, black Franken-
stein shoes, and wife-beaters, they looked like someone's
backup dancers.

"Which one is he?" Diane, one of the other models, whispered to Star.

"I honestly don't know," Star confided with a tiny shrug. "They all look alike. They're all hot."

"I noticed that. Is he in a rock-and-roll band or a marching band?" Missy teased, laughing at her own joke.

"I'm not so sure." Star shrugged. "But it looks as though he's not going to be in here anytime soon."

"Look, Jeeves," Jimi shouted loudly enough to be heard at Star's table. "We are supposed to be meeting guests at your foofy, uptight place. You should be happy we're here. Look around."

"That's him, the belligerent one." Star nodded disgustedly, recognizing the attitude from the fight he'd gotten into when he'd broken into her trailer only a week earlier and surprised yet another intruder who'd beaten him to it.

She smiled at herself.

She had broken up the fight in her trailer and gotten Jimi to leave by promising to go out on a date with him when she got back from Cabo if he stopped stalking her. She also agreed to read a movie script that the other intruder, Steph Golden, had broken in to leave for her. And there she was going out with Jimi in Cabo and she'd not read a word of the *Hy Voltz* script. Not my most successful negotiation, she thought ruefully.

"He seems very, um, persistent," Cindy fished for a compliment as she sipped at the straw in her fruity drink. "That's always a good sign, right?" Her head bobbed back and forth like a tennis spectator's as she watched Jimi trying to outflank the implacable maître d'.

"Yeah," Star said, bemused as security stepped in to prevent Jimi from coming to her table. "You've got to admire his determination."

"Sure, what the fuck?" Kat said, toasting with her coconut shell.

Star rose to rescue him before he wound up in some seedy Mexican jail.

"A man will follow his dick off a cliff." Diane shrugged, stirring her drink with the straw.

"Is there a cliff nearby?" Star called over her shoulder with a little laugh and a toss of her head that brought both Jimi and the security guards up short.

"Hi," Jimi said, twisting his goatee nervously, unable to manage much more than an adolescent croak. "You look fucking amazing."

"Is there a problem?" Star asked without addressing Jimi directly.

"Señorita e'Star," the maître d' fawned. "I am so sorry I did not realize, is this man a guest of yours?"

"Yeah. What's wrong?"

"I'm afraid that the Ritz has a very strict dress code," the maître d' said with an obsequious bow. "I can offer you and your guests a table by the pool perhaps? Or in the cabana? But I cannot allow gentlemen without jackets in the Land's End Club after six. My sincerest apologies."

"No worries," Star said, waving the nervous man in for a landing with a gentle gesture. "Tell you what. I haven't gotten to see much of Cabo. Perhaps you could recommend a nightclub. Something local and not too touristy? Where we could go for a little drink in the company of gentlemen without jackets?"

"I'm sure Miss e'Star could get in anywhere in the world she cared to call," the man said with another bow. "But, perhaps Madre de la Perla?"

"What?" Star asked. The name brought her up short. "What's the name of the place?"

"Madre de la Perla," the man repeated. "In *inglés,* Mother of Pearl. It's an open-air *cantina de la ostra*—oyster bar."

"I'm home," Star said, flinging her arms around Jimi's neck and hopping up and down as she spun him around. "Shuck me, suck me, eat me raw!" she shouted.

"I thought you'd never ask," Jimi said, grinning as he took her in his arms.

"They're actually supposed to be a 'hypochondriac,'" Star explained to her mystified party as she drained the oyster shell of its contents and chased it with a shot of tequila. "That means they'll put lead in your pencil," she added with a confidential giggle. "Who wants an oyster shot?" she asked as she dropped the hollow shell into the gold, spray-painted coffee can that had been placed on their table to collect the empties.

The whole place had the same sort of makeshift feel to it. Formerly a dockside gas station and general store catering to local fishermen, with a little imagination and a lot of spray paint, the place had been converted into a dockside gas station, general store, *and* a bar. There were a few rough wooden tables, benches, and an odd assortment of old webbed lawn chairs, where local fish and seafood were served fresh off the fishing boats that bought gas and shopped for supplies there.

The fiberglass had been stripped from the old red-and-white promotional gas station awning, and the rusty, bare frame had been wound with old, loudly colored Christmas tree lights. Brightly hued scraps of cloth hung from the rafters to separate the *cantina de la ostra* from the Texaco. Local musicians serenaded Star and her party with their brassy music from the deck of a small pontoon boat, lashed alongside the dock.

It was quite perfect. Exactly what Star had been looking for. But it was the name of the establishment that got to her like a message from the universe and her late grandfather Papa Jens that tonight was the right thing to do. As she watched the waitresses, she remembered her life in Miami at Mother Pearl's Steak and Oyster Emporium, where she'd lugged beer and shucked oysters wearing a tiny T-shirt emblazoned with those immortal words: SHUCK ME, SUCK ME, EAT ME RAW. The memory made her smile.

Jimi had entertained by playing all the glasses at the table like drums, smashing most of them. His reckless abandon was appealing somehow, and Star couldn't resist the growing attraction as he tugged her out onto the dance floor. Water misted on them from pinholes in water pipes in the rafters to help keep the dancers cool, and soon the small dance floor was filled with wet, tanned half-naked bodies.

"It's time for instant margaritas," Jimi announced.

"Instant?" Star said, crinkling her nose. "In this place? I think scratch margaritas all you're likely to get."

"No, not instant like that," Jimi said, hopping up on the table and waving the waitress over. "*Un* bottle . . . how do you say *bottle* in *español*?"

"*Botella.*" She smiled.

"Cool. *Una botella* of tequila and *una botella* of triple sec and *una de* lime juice . . . how do you say *lime juice*?"

"*Jugo de cal,*" the waitress, who clearly spoke perfect English, answered.

"*Gracias.*" Jimi nodded, making quite the show of it. "*Una botella* of *jugo de cal, por favor.*"

"Are you going to make margaritas at the table?" Star asked, sure of the recipe for margaritas from her tenure hawking cocktails.

"Sort of," Jimi said. "It's even more instant than that," he explained, opening the bottles and lining them up. "Okay, I'll go first. Star, you're in charge of tequila. Missy, you take the *jugo de cal*. And it's Diane, right?"

"Right." Diane smiled despite herself.

"Diane, you have the easy job," he said, handing her the remaining bottle. "You're on triple sec."

"Jimi," Star said, laughing at the production he was making of the whole thing. "What are we supposed to mix the drinks in?"

"Ah," he said, lying back on the table and letting his head hang off the end as he faced the canopy of garish Christmas lights and stars. "That's what makes them instant margaritas. They don't become margaritas until the instant they touch my tongue."

"Got it." Star laughed.

As Jimi lay back on the table, the girls poured the contents into his mouth. What his Mix-Mistresses lacked in technique, they made up for in enthusiasm and quantity. Most of their first batch wound up on the front of Jimi's shirt. But Jimi was both a willing and eager coach. Before long, the whole cantina was in on it.

Star gave it a try. "Isn't it funny how tequila goes straight to your nipples," she announced as she sat up. Despite the fact that it was a warm night and she was still overheated from the dance floor, they were obviously rock hard.

The night just kept getting stranger. One of Jimi's friend's dimples started to freak her out, and Star had to beg him not to smile. She began analyzing everyone, taking an interest in the strangest things. When she went to the ladies' to freshen up, she was taken by how hot it felt to pee. "I could pee for an hour," she told one of the girls who'd come with her. "That tequila must be really fresh or something."

At one point, Jimi borrowed a skull ring from "Dimples" and made quite the show of proposing, telling everyone who'd listen that Star was every young boy's fantasy, that it was love at first sight. She tried to say no, but he was having none of it, and so she just smiled and enjoyed the feel of the cool silver on her finger.

She didn't know what it was, but the night just kept getting better and better. The colored lights looked more vibrant against that sky. The stars kept getting brighter. The moon was blinding. The drinks couldn't have been tangier. Even the feel of the lawn chair was a treat against her skin.

"Oh, my God," she cried out, rubbing against the webbing. "This chair feels amazing."

Jimi exchanged a look and a laugh with his buds.

"X-cellent," he said, giving Star and his friends the thumbs-up. "Totally x-cellent. Maybe we should go for a walk on the beach, Star." He offered her his hand and she took it, only to marvel at the feel of his skin against hers.

"Your hands are so soft and yet so strong," Star said, rubbing his hand between both of hers. "It feels wonderful."

"And your hands feel awesome on mine," he moaned as she ran her hands up his arms.

The two could barely walk for grasping one another, and

Jimi's posse laughed at their awkward progress across the restaurant toward the beach.

"Ecstasy?" Diane asked elliptically.

Jimi's clones only laughed in reply.

"You fucker," Star said, striking the still-bound Jimi with the flat of her hand on his taut stomach. Like a belly flop it made a bigger noise than anything else. "You slipped me Ecstasy? Is that why I feel so weird?" she demanded, running her hand up and down the smooth naked skin of his stomach. It felt warm and velvety under her palm and she quickly became mesmerized by the sensation.

"Dude, I totally thought you'd have done X before," he said, pleading his case, her touch heating him up but his bonds keeping him from doing anything about the sweet torture of it. "Honest, I would never have slipped you anything if I'd known."

"Is that why I can't remember what happened," she said, tearing her hand away from the irresistible feeling of his skin.

"Well," he admitted, sorry but relieved that she'd stopped her stroking. "There were a number of substances involved. After the instant margaritas you just couldn't get enough."

"So you tricked me?"

"Well, you weren't exactly unconscious."

"But it's the same thing as forcing me," she said, strangely torn between the desire to feel his skin against her hand and her confused outrage at his revelation.

"You're not the one tied to the bed," he pointed out. "Wait and hear the rest of the story before you decide."

"So, you're saying that I wanted to do all these drugs?" Star said, recoiling, her hand clutched to her chest. The feel of her own skin was awesome, not to mention the sensation of her hand touching her naked breasts.

"You wanted a lot more than that," Jimi said with a dirty little laugh.

Their first kiss, though chemically enhanced, was electric and lasted, more or less, for two days. Star thought that there was a magical bond between them, above and beyond the attraction that she already felt.

There was something funny and sweet and, despite his outward ultrahip affectation, kind of nerdy about him. She couldn't quite put her finger on it, but Jimi Deed was charming in a way that made you want to take care of him.

And he knew how to kiss.

The Ecstasy just made her unable to resist more of a good thing.

"Oh, Jimi," she gasped, coming up for air but not really breaking contact with him. "You feel so . . . perfect against me." She groaned as she ground her hips into his.

"God, baby, that feels sooo good!" he howled, throwing his head back.

"Your T-shirt feels like velvet." She shivered, allowing the straps at her shoulders to fall away so that she could brush her bare nipples against the ribbed fabric. "Oh, feel the wind on your skin," Star said, turning and letting the warm sea breeze caress her naked flesh in the privacy of the night-darkened beach.

"You're so warm," he said, wrapping his arms around her

from behind and grinding his denim-encased erection into the silky fabric of the tiny black shorts sliding from her waist.

"I can't explain how I feel," Star said, reaching behind to grasp his thighs and urging him more tightly against her.

"Your body feels great," Jimi said, boldly running his hand up to fondle her breasts with such delicate finesse that there was only enough contact to create an arc of sensation.

Star shivered from the intensity.

Sensations fired through her body. The moist sand under her feet like walking on cooked oatmeal. The froth of the waves lapping at her ankles like lace cuffs. And Jimi's urgent and growing sexual need, like static electric shocks with each touch.

"You know what?" she said, turning back so abruptly that it startled him. "I think getting in the water naked would be so awesome right now. And I have a Jacuzzi in my room." She was so excited she was shouting.

"That is so cool," he said, embracing her, thrilled almost to the point of orgasm by just the idea of being naked in a tub with Star. He could feel himself begin to leak as little spasms rocked his body.

"Race you," she said, breaking away and running up the beach in the direction of the hotel.

Star was tearing off what was left of her clothes even before the door to her room closed. Jimi followed her as she filled the tub and climbed in.

The water felt like warm Jell-O against her skin, thicker somehow. More viscous. And then, Jimi was on her, rubbing against her, and they were naked together for the first time, in the warm, silky water.

His mouth sought hers out and the feeling of his tongue entwined with hers was almost too much. It was as if they were kissing in slow motion as each tried to seek out every bump and serration and indentation in the mouth of the other.

"What does this feel like?" he asked, trailing his fingers down her body and sliding them inside.

Star shrieked. The orgasm was instantaneous, swift, and fierce. Jimi merely brushed against that most sensitive spot and she went off like a gunshot. The effect was so intense she had to hang on to Jimi for support. But unlike a gunshot, it went on and on. As his fingers explored, it just kept happening, rolling over her like waves in a storm, too numerous to count and too frequent to regain her footing.

"Oh, God," she said, when at last she found words. "You've got about two days to stop doing that."

So he did it again.

The effect was exactly the same, or maybe even better, she couldn't decide because he didn't stop the second time until she forced his hand away, unable to endure the pleasure any longer. It was a delicious pain, like drinking something really cold when you're thirsty on a hot day. It burns so good going down. Sex with Jimi was like orgasms came by the gallon and she was drinking too fast.

She pushed him backward until he stumbled and ended up sitting on the enormous tub's silky marble steps. And, like the neck of the Loch Ness monster, his erection broke the surface even though the steps were submerged.

Wow, she thought.

"What?" he asked.

"You know what I'm really good at?" Star asked mischievously.

"What?" He grinned in reply.

"Holding my breath."

She took him into her mouth, her head underwater as she plumbed the depths.

"Oh, shit," his voice rang out in the marble room.

She almost drowned, but what a way to go.

They spent the next two days naked in the water. They rubbed, licked, sucked, fondled, and tasted each other to orgasm so repeatedly that their entire bodies were chapped and raw. After the first couple of hours they had discovered Star's video camera, and they began relentlessly filming each other, not only when they were rubbing each other raw, but in the bathroom or showering or eating breakfast.

They simply could not seem to get enough of each other. It was as though the camera allowed them to see more than just when they were looking at each other.

He was filming her when he said those words that reshaped their destinies.

"Marry me?"

She looked up at him with a nervous giggle and smiled. It was as though she was checking to see if he was kidding.

"Okay," she said.

"And the ring?" she asked, wiggling her upturned fingers.

"We stole it," Jimi admitted.

"Oh my God," Star gasped. It was quite the rock and she knew they'd be looking for it. She tried to pull it from her hand, moving toward the door to throw the ring into the ocean below, but his laughter stopped her. "What's so funny?"

"You," he said. "We didn't steal it. I bought it for you."

"That's not all that funny," she giggled, unable to resist his full and easy laugh.

"No," he admitted, still laughing. "It's not. But you wanted to."

"I did?" she asked in disbelief, crossing back over to him.

"That's why you bought that gun," he said. "I shouldn't have let you, but really, you buying that gun was the best thing ever."

"Excuse me," Star said to the clerk at Salvatore's. "Do you speak English?"

"Si, Señora," he replied, beaming at her. "What do you need today?"

"A gun," she said, looking through the glass case at the revolvers the store had on offer, while Jimi videotaped the scene.

"A gun?" the clerk asked, only a little surprised after years of American tourists. "What sort of gun?"

"I don't know," she shrugged. "The silver one is nice."

"Lo siento, Señora," the clerk corrected himself. "What will you be using the gun for?"

"I need to rob a jewelry store," Star said, looking up from the glass case and smiling into the man's startled face. She had counted on surprising him—and she succeeded.

"The, uh, silver one should be fine," he said, recovering as Jimi's laughter shook the camera. "Perhaps this is a little joke?"

"Oh no, I'm serious," Star assured the man. "Could I hold it?"

"Por supuesto." The clerk gave her a bow, took a key from his pocket, and opened the case. "Here you go," he said, handing her the gun.

"Heavy," she said, assuming her best Charlie's Angels' stance, tossing her hair back and posing both for the camera and for Jimi. "How many thingies does it hold?" she asked, looking down the barrel.

"Siete . . . seven thingies," the clerk said, glad that the gun was not loaded.

"Does it come with thingies?" she asked, sighting the clerk down the barrel.

"No, but we sell thingies as well." He ducked to get a box of bullets from below the counter. "May I?" he asked, extending his hand.

Star handed the clerk the gun, and he demonstrated how to insert the bullets into the magazine.

"Cool," she said. "I'll take it and a dozen of the thingies."

"A dozen?" the clerk asked. "We sell them by the box."

"Yeah, er, right," Star shrugged. "I mean a dozen boxes."

"This must be quite a jewelry store," the clerk said, playing along with the joke as he assembled the purchase.

"It's an amazing ring," Star said, leaning against Jimi. "We're going to be married."

"Congratulations," the clerk said. "Will there be anything else?"

"Does it need batteries?"

"But we didn't rob the store?"

"No, I'd already bought you the ring before you bought

the gun." Jimi smiled, remembering the exhilaration he'd felt in that moment, and pretty much every moment since he'd left with Star for Madre de la Perla.

"And the wedding?"

"At some club." He rolled his eyes. "We got the license and had a Mexican Elvis impersonator marry us after the bikini contest. The winner was your maid of honor. You both wore white."

"Bikinis?"

"Naturally."

"So, how did you get tied up?" she said, zooming in to film his answer.

"You convinced me to let you," he replied with as much of a shrug as he could manage under the circumstances. "It seemed like a good idea at the time. Kind of hot, actually.

"Why didn't I let you go?"

"To keep me from going back to work and leaving you here," he said, looking away.

"You're lying," she said, leaning in, the camera just inches away from the tip of his nose.

"No, I had a big concert I was supposed to do yesterday," he said. "They're pretty pissed. Turn on the news. They're looking all over the world for me."

"But that isn't why I wouldn't let you go, is it?" she said, reaching down and stroking his cock again.

"Don't start that again," he winced. "I'm sore all over after the last few days. Aren't you?"

"I wondered why my nipples hurt," she nodded, the camera bobbing. "So tell. Why wouldn't I untie you?"

"So I wouldn't go back to my girlfriend."

"Your girlfriend?" she said, jumping to her feet and dropping the camera, but not turning it off. "You have a girlfriend? But we're married."

"Maybe," he said. "I'm not sure about ceremonies conducted by Elvis impersonators. He did do a good 'Volare.' "

" 'Volare' isn't an Elvis song," she said petulantly.

"I'm just saying."

"So are we married or aren't we?"

"I think we get to decide that."

"And how do we do that?"

"Watch the tapes," he suggested. "You'll see what I got to see the past few days."

"Why did you ask me to marry you?" she asked, sitting again and placing the camera on the bedside table to film them both.

"We're good together."

"The sex."

"Hell yeah, but that's not it."

"Like what?"

"Like even now, I'm tied to the bed, you're holding me hostage at gunpoint and sitting there naked and, well, I don't know about you, but this just fits."

"I remember," she shrieked, leaping up and jumping on the bed. "I remember, I remember, I remember!"

"Everything?" he said bouncing uncomfortably.

"No," she said, stopping and letting the bed recede. "But I remember why I tied you up."

There was a long silence. She stood over him on the bed, staring out the window.

"Why?" he asked, finally.

"Why what?"

"Why did you tie me up?"

"I can't tell you."

"Why not?" he asked, puzzled.

"I don't know if I can trust you."

"Babe, in the last few days you've told me your whole life."

"Yeah, but I don't remember that. I just remember that you tried to leave me and so I tied you up."

"Because you love me?"

"I hardly know you."

"Because you were afraid to be alone?"

"Not exactly."

"What exactly?"

"Because I feel so at ease with you around," she said, trying to put words to it. "Being naked around you is like wearing a coat and gloves on a cold day."

"But you're Miss March," he said a little surprised. "And the world's favorite lifeguard."

"Being an exhibitionist is the best cover for being shy," Star said, reaching up to brush his long black hair away from his face. "No one suspects."

He turned his head to kiss her hand as she stroked his hair. They regarded each other a moment.

"What's left to hide?" he asked her.

"Me," she said simply. "The part I save for myself."

He shook his head, not understanding.

"There's this website," she said, folding her hands in her lap and looking out the window of the room. "This guy spends his whole life following me around and taking pictures of me and posting them on this website. It's like his career or something. He has pictures of me going to work.

Pictures of me going to the store. Pictures of me walking the dog, on the set, having lunch with friends, on dates, kissing, holding my mother's hand. He even has pictures of me sleeping. It's like he's stealing my life. Not the part that we all give the world, but the part I keep for me." The tears felt warm on her face.

They sat silent for a long time. Jimi looked at Star and she looked out the window at the late-afternoon light reflecting on the ocean below.

"Untie me," he said at last.

"So can you escape?"

"So I can hold you."

Star looked at Jimi a moment. Maybe he was telling the truth. Or maybe she just wanted to be held. Either way, she couldn't make much of a marriage out of it if she kept her husband tied to the bed. Eventually they'd have to change the sheets.

Looking around for something to cut the bonds with, Star spied some dagger-sized shards of glass from the table she'd shot earlier. She wrapped one of them in a towel so she wouldn't cut her hands, then sawed through the random bonds she couldn't untie or unbuckle.

"If you love something, let it go," she said, stepping back from the bed when he was free.

"I always thought that was such a stupid thing," he said, rubbing his wrists. "I mean, if you let it go, how will it know you love it?"

She laughed, still a little woozy from the afternoon and God knew what all else.

Jimi extended his arms and Star fell into them.

It was just them, naked in bed with a blender. No Ecstasy,

no special effects, just the two of them joined perfectly together like interlocking pieces in a puzzle.

Jimi ran his hands down her body, drawing her so tightly
into him it was as if he were trying to merge them into one.
When they kissed, it was the same. It wasn't just sex, it was as
if they were trying to become one person, two halves fused together. When she took him in her mouth, or he was inside her,
the passion turned them into a single being, if only for a perfect instant.

When it was done, they lay sweating together, still united,
unwilling to separate. Star writhed against her husband, moving to excite him, to extend their union and . . . and that's
when she heard the noise, the excruciatingly familiar sound of
a camera's auto rewind. She saw only a man's shoe under the
curtains. That's all she needed before she was up, gun in hand,
running for the balcony.

"You son of a bitch!" she screamed, running toward the
sound. The shoe disappeared and she saw the man run for
the rope ladder he must have used to climb down from the
rooftop onto her balcony.

Jimi was too blissed out to realize what was going on, but
when he heard Star's shouts and screams he followed her out
onto the balcony, where he found her holding a gun on a man
hanging from the railing—dangling, really—hundreds of feet
above the jagged rocks of the coastline below.

"Get the camera," she directed.

"What's going on?" Jimi asked, unsure of what he was
witnessing or what he should do.

"This is the guy," Star said by way of explanation, brush-
ing away angry tears. "You know . . . this is the one with the
website."

"Star?" Jimi said, unsure of what she wanted.

"It's time for a little confession," she said, prodding the photographer's ribs with the toe of her Gucci boot. "Get the camera."

A smile split Jimi's face. "You got it, babe."

He returned with the camera, and the two spent the next few minutes forcing the intruder to admit what he was doing and how he got into his present predicament. While the man pleaded for his life, Star got his name and ID as a souvenir.

Satisfied, they were at a loss for what to do next.

The idea seemed to occur to the two of them at once.

"On three?" Jimi said, taking her hand in his.

Star nodded.

"One," they said together, each peeling a finger from the railing as Jimi continued to film. "Two . . ." Another finger. "Three!"

With a scream and a wail the man fell from view, past the twenty stories of the hotel, down the cliffs and into the rocks hundreds of feet below. The crashing waves swept him out to sea.

Jimi filmed for a while, unable to think of anything else.

Star scanned nearby balconies to determine whether anyone had witnessed the photographer's fall.

They looked at each other. Did anyone see? Did anyone hear? Dare they breathe?

And with that thought came a pounding on the door.

"Oh shit," Star said.

"Get the tapes," Jimi instructed as they dashed back into the room.

Star raked their videos into a pillowcase and knotted it.

More pounding.

She stepped awkwardly into a pair of bikini bottoms and barely grabbed the top while Jimi, clad only in a pair of jams and a tank, grabbed her hand and dragged her out onto the balcony.

As the knocking continued, they climbed the photographer's rope ladder up to the roof and pulled it up behind them, just as the door to their room opened.

"Room service," the maid called from the door. "Ay, dios mio."

2

sweet peace
and time

How did I get here? Star wondered as she looked around the harbor at Cannes. Dressed in formal black rubber, laced up the front, and cinched at the waist, she rode at the prow of a yacht the movie studio had hired to create her entrance at the film festival. She was excited about attending. She was excited about being in the movie. She'd read the script for *Hy Voltz* with Jimi and fallen in love with the idea of being an action hero. The studio had been amazing, putting everything together. It helped take away a little of the fear she felt about being catapulted up onto the big screen.

But that morning truly took her breath away.

To this almost too perfect small town on the ocean were added that morning the perfect mix of fluffy white clouds and sunshine, a gentle breeze, and hundreds, possibly thousands, of smaller boats dotting the harbor, each laden with photographers and video crews poised to capture the moment of Star's arrival at that year's film festival.

How had this happened?

She laughed as she waved at the well-wishers and paparazzi who bobbled in her wake. She looked up at Jimi, who sat next to the captain on the bridge, and shared a secret smile as if to confide a bit of her disbelief.

They exchanged a wary glance. Ever since Cabo they'd been looking over their shoulders. The body of the photographer who had fallen from their hotel balcony had washed ashore in Migrino, just up the Baja coast. There had been speculation about his death, but most thought he'd simply fallen scaling the cliffs in search of his prey. And it really was that simple, he had fallen. But Jimi and Star were a little paranoid about hiding out since their marriage had made them the targets of even more media attention. Plus, Jimi was being sued for missing the show, though insurance was covering it.

Their secret, not to mention their tormentors, had provided them with a common enemy. They became inseparable. So when Star had accepted the movie role and the promotional debut at Cannes, Jimi was right there at her side.

He grinned.

It was all the encouragement that she needed. She turned back to the crowds and the eyes of the world and waved. She could hear the shouts and cheers over the roar of the massive engines that powered her toward the red carpet that had been rolled out all the way down to the water's very edge to receive her.

She felt a strange swelling inside, as though she might cry

or run for cover. Perhaps it was joy or pride or ego or just fear or paranoia or a little bit of all of the above. She stood alone on the deck of a ship arriving in a city where she had never before been to promote a film that had not even been shot or, for that matter, even fully scripted. But here was the world waiting to welcome her, watching her every move. It was her they had come to see, and she knew it for sure for the first time that perfect morning, she just didn't know why.

The weeks with Jimi leading up to Cannes had been a whirlwind. Like a honeymoon on crack. They had returned from Cabo to Jimi's Malibu beachfront of a bachelor pad. The multimillion-dollar home was still only sparsely furnished with a few well-chosen pieces and some art. Warhol's pink camouflage hung above the bed, which was just a mattress on the floor, albeit a really, really nice mattress. A bedsheet partially covered the plate-glass window with the money-shot view of the golden sands of Malibu.

"Were you robbed?" Star asked warily as she regarded the interior of their new home. "The morons. Isn't that a Warhol?"

Jimi laughed, sluicing through the art and architecture books. "When my ex-girlfriend left, I told her to take what she wanted, and she wanted a lot. I just haven't gotten around to it. But, this way we can make it our own. It won't be like you're moving into my place, it'll really be ours."

"Yeah, I guess," Star said, realizing how little she knew about this man. "It's my favorite Warhol ever."

"Then I must have bought it for you," he said quietly. And then, "Oh, dude!" he exclaimed suddenly, striking himself on the forehead. "I totally spaced on this one." Without further explanation or intimation, he dragged Star out the front door, swept her into his arms, and carried her, not only across the threshold but back up the stairs and to the mattress by the window in his bedroom.

As they tore the sheets from the window, the magic of sunset poured into the room, and the spartan surroundings were forgotten as the forces of their need for each other once again overpowered them.

He couldn't get inside her fast enough.

"Oh, hell, yeah." Jimi heaved, driving himself inside her. It had been all the time since the hotel room in Cabo that they'd had their last fix, and both were glad the wait was over.

Star clawed at his back, matching his urgency as she tore at him.

It was beautiful, efficient sex, and both were taken care of more than once before the sun slipped below the horizon. If true love is when you come at the same time, this was it always.

Jimi fell away and they lay gasping, bathed in sweat and the pinkish gray twilight that spilled up from the ocean below and poured over the room through the massive unmasked window.

"I do love a good sunset," Star sighed contentedly.

She awoke to the harsh glare of morning from the unshaded window.

She clasped the sheet around her as she arose and then giggled as she realized what she was doing. In truth, it was stranger for the pair to be dressed in each other's company than nude.

Laughing, she cast the sheet aside and bounded out of bed to find her husband. As she padded down the second-floor landing, which was in effect the upstairs hallway, she heard Jimi singing the lyrics to "Rapper's Delight."

Following the sound of his voice, Star walked naked through several expansive but otherwise unidentifiable empty rooms.

She sang back to him, joining in the words to the song.

"In here, honey pie," his voice came from behind a pair of double swinging doors.

She smiled as she passed through the mahogany doors and into a vast commercial-scaled kitchen, all stainless steel and black tile. At the far side, bent over a range larger than the one they had back at Mother Pearl's, was her new husband.

"What are you doing?" she asked as she made her way around the archipelago of utility islands that dotted the un-fathomable interior of the immense room. "And what's with this room? Will we be shooting a cooking show or are we opening a cafeteria?"

"Bowling alley," he said, still not looking at her.

"Too big." She laughed. "We'll never find the balls. So what's up? Coffee?"

"Ta-dah," he proclaimed, wheeling to greet her, stark naked and presenting a rather splendid breakfast tray. "The most important meal of the day—breakfast."

She dissolved into fits of laughter as she looked at the tray.

"You can cook!" Star said with delight, clapping her hands, pleased to know something practical about him. In fact, pleased to know anything about him at all.

"Let's eat outside," he suggested, strolling out of the house onto the patio.

"And do the neighbors care that we're not formally dressed?" Star asked, following him out to the pool.

"It's one of the reasons I got this place," he explained, setting out the food on a wrought-iron table near the pool. "It's right next to a nature preserve on one side and a cliff on the other. So there are no neighbors."

Star had to admit that he was a very good cook. Granted, fruit, fried eggs, and toast weren't that challenging, but nothing was burned and the presentation was imaginative. The two grapefruit halves had cherries in the center. "Hmm," she said, holding them up to her chest. "Freudian. Got something on your mind?"

"Just breastfast," he grinned.

"It's a great house." Star looked around for a chair to pull up to the iron table. "Lots of potential," she added, mentally decorating the place when Jimi leaped abruptly into the pool, reemerging with first one, and then a second wrought-iron chair to match the table. Placing each on the deck, he leaped adroitly from the water and made his way over to Star with the chairs. More amazing to her than his behavior was the fact that the chairs actually matched the table.

"What else is down there?" she asked, peering tentatively over the side.

"Not much now," Jimi shrugged. "For a couple of weeks there was a 1967 Cadillac convertible after a kick-off party we had for one of our albums, I forget which."

"Whose car?" she asked, taking her chair. The wet iron was chilly against her bare skin.

"Not sure," he said, toying with the left grapefruit. "Seems almost painful to break up the set now."

She gave a little rumble of laughter. "So, how'd the car wind up there?"

"Parking," he said with a vague air.

Breakfast in the warm morning sun was easy and pleasant; their worries were soon forgotten as they laughed and talked together.

"Do you want anything else?" he asked as the plates were pushed aside.

"Umm-hmm," Star grinned, slipping under the table and taking him in her mouth.

Jimi was impressed with Star's place. It was filled with French antiques. Though some, like the "real Parisian sidewalk," were of dubious origin, none was of the distressed and pickle-white American type. It was girly, but he had to admit it was well put together. Lots of cool stuff like the PlayStation and the big-screen TV, an excellent stereo system, video game system, and lots of furniture that was more about how it felt than how it looked. And it looked great. Too much pink for his taste, but otherwise, a thumbs-up. And two thumbs-up for the fully stocked bar that he hit hard.

Star was relieved to be home for the first time in three weeks. She immediately called Engel, her buddy from the *Lifeguards* crew who was dog-sitting with Mutley, to check on her beloved pooch and to get him over to the house as soon as possible. Then she hit the showers to wash off what was left of Cabo.

Jimi snooped around a bit, getting to know more about her, but if you look for something long enough, you'll find it.

He had been looking for more game cartridges. What he found was a drawer full of men's clothes.

Star had decided that the shower was not quite enough and was just sinking into a tub full of gardenia-scented bubbles when the door to the bathroom flew open and Jimi began emptying the drawer full of clothes into the tub with her.

"What the hell are these?" he demanded.

"Um, I don't know," Star said, unsure of just how to react.

"The question is, whose clothes are these?" Jimi screamed, leaning down closer as though she might not hear him.

"Is there some kind of prize?" Star asked, trying for humor.

"You think this is funny?"

"Not anymore," she sighed, getting out of the tub full of wet clothes and crushed gardenia bubbles. "So what's the problem, Jimi?"

"They're men's clothes!" he leaned in and shouted again.

"Yeah?" Star said, losing patience. "Come on, you think you're the first?"

She shoved her way past and stepped back into the shower to wash off the remains of her ruined bubble bath.

Jimi was stunned and chastened. Her complete lack of intimidation or even reaction to his bullying startled him.

"I'm sorry, hon, it just freaked me out," he said, sitting on the side of the tub, still holding the drawer.

"Duh," her voice echoed inside the shower.

Jimi didn't know exactly what to do. With his ex-wife there had never really been anything to deal with. She'd done things pretty much her way, and he'd either gone along or been left behind. They'd never really fought, but then they'd never really talked either. She'd never given him reason to be jealous, and frankly, he'd never really paid her that much attention.

"Look, Jimi," Star said gently, emerging from the shower. "I'm in love with you. I've never felt like this before. And I can't explain it. But I don't know a damned thing about you. And you don't know anything about me. This is just something to know about me. Did I see other men before we met? Yes. But it's over now, I married you. The end. Okay?"

"Okay," Jimi said, taking the towel from her and gently drying her off.

"Did you?"

"See other men before we met?" Jimi asked.

She laughed.

"I've taken full advantage of being a rock star. I've been mostly single for the past two years," he said with a little shrug. "I had a serious girlfriend. And I was married. Twice."

"Really? Well, then, you already know how this works."

"If I did I'd still be married, right?"

She laughed. "So, does it bother you that I've been with other men?"

"No," he shrugged. "When I think about it, it seems kind of hot. Like I'd like to watch."

"Yeah," she giggled, and then caught his eye and stopped. "Really?"

"Yeah." He grinned. "Like live porn."

"We can do anything we want," she said, climbing onto his lap and licking the side of his face as he'd done to her the first time they met. "Anything?"

They laughed at their shared secret for a moment, and then he buried his face in her breasts.

The doorbell rang.

"Mutley!" Star shouted, snatching a robe from the hook behind the bathroom door. "Mutley's home. Why don't you

clean this mess up and then come meet the only competition
you've got."

The wet towel smacked him on the side of the head.

The pictures were a sensation. The shots of two of them,
breakfasting naked at Jimi's, Star's feet sticking out from
under the table, her head in his lap, began appearing on the
cover of every questionable publication on the planet, and
even a few fairly respectable ones, almost before they'd done
the dishes.

Star was at a loss.

The press had always been persistent, but this was a whole
new dimension. This kind of coverage was like breaking and
entering. Jimi took it even worse than she did. They'd been
walking back to Star's after breakfast at The Omelet Shoppe
when they'd passed a newsstand virtually plastered with the
pictures. They froze for a second as they realized what they
were seeing. And then Jimi began railing and shredding the
papers and magazines.

Of course, the next day, everything at that and every other
newsstand was covered with pictures of him tearing up the
pictures the day before. Even more chilling was that neither
had had any idea they were being watched. The secret
weighed on them more.

In a way, it began to bond them together. At a time when
they were looking for common ground on which to build
their relationship, the constant perception that they were
being watched and pursued bound them together as nothing
else could have. It was "us against them."

Even in the first few days of their marriage, it became clear that more was afoot than simply the normal attention and curiosity surrounding a celebrity couple.

They were besieged.

One benefit was that there was never any wait for the official garbage pickup. All the trash was stolen within minutes of its being put out by the curb. The downside was that within days the press was filled with even more "trash" about them than usual, from speculation about their carb and alcohol consumption to their magazine subscriptions and product preferences.

Star then hired a private service to clean the house, as well as shred, destroy, and haul away all the "evidence."

The afternoon before the cleaning crew was scheduled, Jimi insisted that Star come with him to their place at the beach.

"There's something I want to show you," he said. "Besides, what else do you have planned?"

It was true. When they weren't making love, they were spending every waking moment together. Jimi even went with her to Skip and Billy's to get her hair done. The only reason Star hadn't wanted to go was because it meant more spy pictures and lurking "reporters."

As it turned out, there didn't seem to be anyone around, and Mutley greatly enjoyed his first visit to their new home. The three of them got into a game of tossing the round cardboard insert from an empty pizza box.

"Ewwww," Star had groaned when Jimi pulled the disk out of one of the empty boxes stacked and awaiting the cleanup crew.

"Relax," Jimi guffawed. "It was a cheese pizza."

Star was too amused to resist, and they played until nearly sundown.

"Mutley is falling for you too," Star said as they made their way back up to the house from the beach.

"Then my evil plan is working," Jimi said, twirling an imaginary mustache and laughing a sinister laugh.

"So, what is it that you wanted to show me?" Star asked, hugging him around the waist as they walked. "This cardboard disk is special, but I'm thinking that we could have ordered in back at the other house."

"Oh, yeah," Jimi said, picking up his pace. "I was having such a good time I almost forgot. The safe."

"What?"

"Well, what with the cleaning crew coming tomorrow," he explained as he led her into the garage, "I just thought it would be a good idea to lock things up. And I figured you should know about the safe too. In case you ever needed it."

The garage had been semiconverted into a practice space for the band. The walls had been lined with carpet-covered baffles to muffle the sound on the outside and improve it on the inside of what was otherwise just a concrete box.

"Over here," he said, taking her to a spot just behind his keyboards. "Put your hand right in here." He guided her hand into a fold in the carpet and she felt the handle and instinctively pulled it.

The false wall swung away to reveal the door of a rather large safe that had been set into the wall behind it.

"Jeez, Jimi. That's huge. I thought it was going to be like one of those wall safes behind a picture that you see in the movies."

"Nah," Jimi chuckled. "You can't put anything in them. And besides, they're too easy to steal."

"Steal?"

"Yeah, you just cut 'em out of the wall and take 'em home to break into at your leisure. This baby," he said, patting the huge, black steel door, "this is here to stay. You'd need a crane and a Mack truck to get it out of here. Leastwise, that's what it took to put it in. Now here's the combination."

Star practiced opening the safe a couple of times until she was proficient.

"And here we go," Jimi said, swinging wide the door to reveal a closet-sized space. There was even a light inside. "It's fireproof and waterproof. So I keep things like family photos and important papers in here. My gun collection. Masters from some of the band's albums. Stuff like that."

"And here I thought it was going to be filled with gold bullion and uncut diamonds," Star said, charmed to find the safe filled mostly with items of sentimental value.

"Nope." He shook his head. "Hell, we don't even have wedding rings."

Mutley lost interest and began exploring the largely empty house, which was like buried treasure as he went sniffing from room to room. Eventually Star came looking for him, but not before he'd had quite the time of it. To Mutley, the house was perfect and Star and Jimi's plans would ruin everything.

"Come on, you," she said, wrestling Mutley out of the empty hall in which she'd envisioned a dining room once the *Hard Luck* album-tour loadout stored there could be relocated. Mutley, who was not going to be taken so easily, had spent the last few hours exploring the huge, empty house and was prepared for quite the game of hide-and-seek, slipping away from Star and taking off.

Star chased him from room to room, finding herself in

what would make a nice nursery one day. Away from the street and the pool, the room had loads of windows, a southern exposure, and more camping equipment than she'd seen in one place outside of the sporting goods section at the Wal-Mart back home in Sunrise City.

She was amazed. In this house, where it seemed no one lived, and with this man who seemed to have no interests outside of his music and the party, here was a room devoted to what, exactly?

"Jimi?" she called. "Jimi, what is all this stuff?"

No answer.

"Jimi," she called, returning to the central atrium and hallway, her voice echoing throughout the house.

She heard a muffled sound, and a moment or so later, Jimi came into the hall in reply.

"What is all this stuff?" she asked, pointing toward the door.

"Oh, it's my Y2K preparedness room." Jimi shrugged. "It seemed like a good idea at the time."

"Camping at the end of the world." She smiled, remembering all the fuss.

"Sounds like a song lyric," he said, picking up the words and singing them to her. "Camping at the end of the world, that's where we could just be."

"Not a bad idea," she said, leaning down to pat Mutley, who'd brought her a tent stake he'd found. "We might get some privacy there."

"You think?" he said, excited by the idea. "What do you think about houseboats?"

"I grew up on an island," she said with a little laugh. "I drove a boat before a car."

"Let's do it. I know the perfect place."

"When?"

"How about now?"

If Jimi had been unsure he loved her before that moment—and he had not been—he knew it for sure right then.

It was the perfect plan.

They would go away for a few isolated days together, and by the time they returned, the house would be ready to begin the renovations. Meanwhile, Star and Jimi had a project and a secret plan and they were ready to depart within twenty-four hours of their decision to go. They told no one, they would simply go missing.

On the evening before their disappearance, Jimi took Star for sushi at Matsuhisa Miyasi's on Sunset Boulevard.

Best of all, though, the famous sushi bar was just down the street from Reggie's. Little more than a trailer on stilts hanging off the side of the ridge that shelved Sunset Boulevard, Reggie's was directly across the street from what for years had been rock and roll's unofficial headquarters, the Sunset Hilton. The often-renovated old hotel had been home to every rock-and-roll band to play every venue on the Strip. Owing to the strategic location and his natural talent, Reggie had become the personal ink artist to the stars and Reggie's one of the most privately famous tattoo parlors in the world.

"Okay," Jimi said over champagne after dinner. "I brought you here for a reason."

"To get me plastered on champagne and take advantage of me?" Star giggled as the bubbles tickled her nose. " 'Cause if you did, you blew it, you're way more plastered than I am."

"No, that's only part of my plan for world domination," Jimi said, taking her hand and kneeling beside their table. "I don't think we ever did this properly. Star," he said, looking at her with such naked sincerity that she fell silent, "I knew the first moment I met you, and I'm more sure every day, that I love you and I want you to be my wife."

"I, um, am." Star said, puzzled.

"Yeah, but we need wedding bands," he said, still kneeling.

"Oh Jimi," she smiled, wagging the huge diamond on her finger. "This ring is plenty for me."

"Well, I was thinking that just a ring, well, that's not permanent. Besides, what ring would ever be beautiful enough for your hand anyway?" he asked as they made their way down the boulevard. "And any ring we got would be the same as thousands of other rings on the fingers of thousands of other people. And then I knew. Permanent, original, and beautiful enough to be on your finger? It had to be Reggie's," he concluded, opening the door to the tattoo parlor.

"Jimi," Reggie called, looking up from the ass of the young woman he was inking with a rather sizable butterfly.

"A tattoo?" Star said. With only one small tattoo on her instep, she wasn't quite the expert.

Now, Jimi had more drawings on him than a subway station in Spanish Harlem. She was taken with the originality of it, and then it hit her.

"Just our names around our fingers," she said. "It's perfect, I love it. Bring it on, Reggie."

Later, as they made their way into a nearby club for a couple of celebratory drinks, they had their double-ring ceremony as they flipped off the press with their newly inscribed ring fingers. Of course the pictures wound up in the papers, but somehow it mattered less.

"Where are you taking me?" she asked, catching Jimi in the viewfinder of their trusty video cam as he merged their SUV onto the freeway and headed east. She hadn't bothered to ask where they were going; it didn't much matter to her as long as they were going together.

"We're heading for London Bridge," he declared, checking over his shoulder and weaving his way left as he picked up speed.

"London Bridge, huh?" she said skeptically. "We're driving to London to go boat camping?"

"Not a bit." He grinned. "Though I'd be really stoked to go up the Thames and the canals on one of those skinny English houseboats. We should totally do that. You can tour the whole country on the canal system they built before they invented trains. They call them narrowboats. They used to be pulled by horses that walked along towpaths they built on the canal banks. It was like a wonder of the world at the time. A single horse could pull a hundred tons. Now they preserve them like parks. We should go."

She never ceased to be amazed by the information that came spewing out of him. With all his *dude*s and *babe*s and *awesome*s and *totally*s he came off as one of the lesser bulbs on the marquee. But his knowledge could be blinding if you flipped the right switch. He had already gotten her a computer, set it up, taught her how to use it, and gotten her online. Not to mention designing and building his own sound studio, doing much of the electronics work himself. In complete contrast to the metal maniac he showed the world, he was a total tech geek, a Boy Scout, and regular Cliff

Clavin about a whole range of topics, like the canals in England.

"Hey," he said, reaching to his waistband and popping his fly. "Check this out."

His erection sprung free of his pants and he stroked it a couple of times for effect.

"Party ready, twenty-four/seven."

"Let's see if I can zoom in enough so people can see that at home," Star teased, zooming in on the formidable erection.

"That's not right, babe," Jimi snorted with indignation. "They can see this from home without a camera."

"I think I'm picking up something." Star giggled, leaning in toward her subject.

"You just need a closer look," Jimi said, taking the camera from her and pushing her head down.

Star had developed some oral talent over the years, and with Jimi's big cock she had really honed her skills. She took a dive and went face-to-face with his shaved balls, swallowing the sword whole.

"Oh, God, babe, you're the best," he said, filming her progress as he continued to rocket them down the freeway into the desert and toward London Bridge.

According to the Guinness book of world records, at $2.4 million the London Bridge was, at the time of its sale, the costliest antique ever purchased. But more outrageous than the price was that it was moved from London, where it had spanned the Thames River for over 140 years, and plopped down across a narrow part of Lake Havasu in the Arizona desert.

"There it is," Jimi said, pointing out the landmark as they cruised across the bridge toward their destination. "London Bridge. You owe me a blow job."

"How can it be London Bridge if it's in Lake Havasu City, Arizona?" Star said, folding her arms defiantly.

"They brought it here brick by brick from London," Jimi said triumphantly, slowing as they made their way through the faux-English tourist trap on the other side.

"I understand that," Star said firmly. "But what made it *London* Bridge was that it was in London, not the bricks it's made out of. Now that it's here, it's Havasu Bridge."

Soon he pulled the car onto the highway that would lead them down the banks of the massive lake to Smackwater Jack's landing, where they'd hired a boat for the weekend. The place was a sort of all-purpose marina for the busy, tasteless tourist on the go. Gas station, grocery store, car park, restaurant, and souvenir shop all under one corrugated-steel roof over a cement-slab floor. The floating docks were covered with bright green AstroTurf that in no way blended in with the muted hues of the desert surrounding them. Best of all, the only news anyone cared about was the weather report. No self-respecting paparazzi was within a hundred miles of the place.

Jack was short for *Jacqueline,* and Smackwater had inherited the place from her Native American father. They'd had to close the rattlesnake zoo after an incident a few years back, but she'd kept the family tradition and the family name alive. Jimi had first seen the place when he was a kid and his family had stopped in to see the rattlesnake zoo. He'd seen the houseboats then and thought what a perfect party they'd make.

And when his garage band had turned into superstars and he could afford to party anywhere he wanted, he'd come back to Smackwater Jack's. It was a great spot for a private party. Jack had respected his privacy and Jimi had paid for the damages. It was the perfect combination.

Much to Star's delight and surprise, after they'd loaded all of Jimi's equipment on board and parked and locked the car, they were on their own.

Jimi knew the lake, or so it seemed to Star, and they were soon in the eerie moonscape surroundings of a massive lake in the middle of the desert. Bounded by stark rock formations carved by the Colorado River, the place felt to Star as though they were boating in the Grand Canyon. The peaks of the canyons and arroyos that had been flooded to contain the eighteen-thousand-acre lake thrust up through the lake's surface at odd angles like broken glass, forming improbable islands as forbidding as mountaintops.

They had been out about an hour and had lost sight of all signs of civilization when Jimi cut the engine. The boat, aside from a slight drift, hung motionless in the middle of the vast lake.

"What is it? Why are we stopping?" she asked.

"This is the deepest point in the lake," he said, catching and holding her eye as the boat rocked in its own wake.

"Here?" she said.

"Here," he nodded.

They dug into the gear and pulled out the huge duffle bag, dragging it to the edge of the deck.

"He's heavy," Star said, as she helped pull the deadweight toward the water.

"He wasn't really," Jimi laughed as they dropped the bag.

"I put weights in it so it would sink to the bottom. Okay, together on three."

"One, two," they chanted together. "Three."

They rolled the bag into the lake and watched it sink, leaving only a few bubbles on the surface in memory.

"Okay, now for the best part." He stood up, pulled his shirt over his head, and shucked his pants. "Freedom," he said with a contented sigh.

"You mean . . ." Star's eyes lit up.

"We won't see anyone and no one will see us," he said with a wink and a nod. "If someone's coming, you'll be able to tell." He gestured at the wide expanse of water on all sides of them.

"Woo, hoo," Star howled, leaping from her seat on the prow and twirling her shirt over her head as she danced a little dance of freedom.

And for the most part, that's how they spent the next ten days. At one point three menacing black helicopters flew silently overhead like huge metal dragonflies as they lay naked on the deck of the boat below. Again, the fear that they had been seen swept over Star like a chill. But the helicopters took no heed of the tourists below, leaving Star and Jimi on their own. No one heard from them and they didn't hear from anyone. No press, no photographers, no agents, no nothing. In fact, if they hadn't brought the camera, there would have been no proof that they were ever there. They were on their own. It was a cherished vacation. By day, they swam and sunned and made love on every flat surface in the boat—and some of the slanted ones too. By night, they pulled the boat into private coves, cooked over fires Jimi built, and slept under the stars.

It was the happiest they would ever be.

Jimi, the gadget fiend, was once again possessed by Star's little video camera and began obsessively documenting their every move. From Star—who'd smoked only one joint ever in her entire life—awkwardly learning to roll joints, to their opus sex cookbook featuring the BreakFuck sandwiches with extra wiener, Ten Inch T-Bones, and Don't-Forget-Where-You-Came-From Mac and Cheese, Jimi got it all on tape. And of course, he captured a scene or two of their lovemaking, including one particularly adventurous session at the ship's helm.

Jimi had been lazily guiding the boat south toward the dam. Star had blended up some fresh strawberry-daiquiri antidote for the afternoon heat. "I have a surprise for you," she called as she climbed up the ladder from the lower deck.

"It's the miracle cure," Jimi said, letting go of the wheel with one hand and taking up the camera to capture her rising from the lower deck, like a blond Venus. He honked the horn with his dick in appreciation of her efforts. He was paying more attention to Star than to steering, the boat lurched, and Star's naked body was covered with strawberry daiquiris.

Never one to be wasteful, Jimi began licking the sweet, sticky nectar off her, following the ruby rivulets of melting ice down her body. Lower and lower, he followed the strawberry trails until they converged in the valley created by her thighs. The daiquiris forgotten and the camera nearly slipping from his hands, Jimi drove his tongue into her hungrily. Star caught the camera and then nearly dropped it again as his tongue hit home and she was hit with her own ecstatic waves. The camera, still running, wound up wedged on a console in front of the throttle, capturing all as Jimi drove Star mad with his attentions.

She cast her head back and held on to Jimi's head as much to support herself as to encourage him as she grew dizzy and light-headed from the heat of the afternoon and Jimi's fevered attentions.

"Yes, oh, damn it, yeah," Star screamed as she wound her fingers into his hair.

At last, able to stand it no longer, she grasped his shoulders, drawing him up to her and pleading with him for release. He was lost in his passion and drove himself mercilessly into her again and again with such force that Star had to hold on to the throttle to avoid being knocked off the console and falling to the deck below.

The throttle thus engaged, the boat's wheel got kicked, steering the boat hard to port so that they began making left turns at full speed. The boat made crazy circles around and around as the wails of its occupants rose and crescendoed. It was like a very adult theme-park thrill ride, spinning around and around as the passion of the moment took them both. The only thing missing was costumed characters.

Spent, they lay in each other's arms on the floor as their world continued to spin around them.

Eventually the camera and boat were switched off, and the two continued to feast on their daiquiris and each other as they lay in the warm spring sun.

"You know what?" he said coyly, flicking at one of her nipples idly with his thumb.

"Not yet," she pleaded, too blissed out in the moment to want to stir herself for another round.

"No, not yet," he agreed, taking a nibble. "I was just going to say that it was these that I first fell in love with."

"What?" She half-laughed.

"Your nipples." He tweaked one between a thumb and a forefinger. "When I saw a magazine photo of them poking holes through your sweater."

She laughed at the idea. The photos were just work for her, so she never thought about them as sexy.

"A, E, I, O, U," she said, laughing.

"What the fuck?" Jimi asked, amused but confused.

"It's what they had me say when they were taking the gatefold shots of me for *Mann* magazine. Supposed to make your mouth look sexy." She laughed harder. "They said, 'Say the vowels,' and I said, 'A, E, I, O, U, and sometimes Y.' "

He was laughing with her.

"But that's not the funniest," she went on. "Mars has this thing about pussy hair. It's his little kink—I guess he misses the seventies—and since he's the publisher, what he likes is what he gets. And he likes girls with a little hair down there. Well, I don't really have any."

"Thank you." Jimi chuckled.

"Just naturally, and I don't encourage what's there." She shrugged. "So Mars saw the test shots and ordered a two-week halt so that I'd have time to grow some. But he could wait the rest of my life and he'd never get what he was looking for from me. Anyway, we waited, and when it came time to go back into the studio, what do you know, I still didn't have any," she said, laughing harder.

"As if having a roomful of strangers talking about the hair on my twat wasn't humiliating enough, they decided they'd get me some. So, they brought in this little old man who specialized in making fake beards and mustaches, and I had to lie on a table like I was at the doctor's office while this poor little man crawled between my legs and glued crepe hair onto me so I'd look like I had something I don't and Mars would get whatever it was that he was looking for."

Jimi couldn't stop laughing.

"So I'm lying there, wrenching my spine, dislocating a shoulder, with a beard glued to my coochie, going, 'A, E, I, O, U, and sometimes Y.' "

They lay in each others arms until their laughter became a quiet periodic rumble.

The afternoon of their last day on the lake, Star and Jimi pulled into one of the lakeside gas stations to fill up as they'd done often enough before. But this time would be different.

During the day the station was run by a lone jockey, Earl, who pumped gas and took money. Business was slow enough that he could usually manage on his own. Besides, it wasn't as if a boat could get very far if a customer decided not to pay. The atmosphere at the gas station was as informal as Earl's uniform. Twentysomething, with shaggy sun-bleached hair and a permanently peeling nose, Earl had long ago torn the sleeves off the light blue attendant's shirt embroidered with his name, which he wore with cut-offs and beat-up sneakers with no socks. Earl had clearly been checking Star out on previous visits, so when she emerged completely naked and strolled over to say hello, she and Jimi knew they had a captive audience.

"How's it going?" she asked.

Earl stood frozen to the spot. It was Miss March. And she was talking to him.

"Uh, fine," he answered, his voice cracking.

"Kinda hot today for all those clothes," Star said, running her hand inside his loosely buttoned shirt.

"Yep," Earl said, not talking about the weather.

"What time do you get off?" Star asked suggestively, her hand sliding slowly down toward his waistband. "Wanna go for a ride?"

"What about your husband?"

"I'm pretty hot too," Jimi said, stepping up behind Star and trailing his fingers up her naked body.

"So, you coming?" Star asked Earl again. "I bet I can cool you both off."

"I get off at sundown," Earl managed to say at last.

"Tonight sundown is just the beginning," Star said, withdrawing her hand and slipping it through Jimi's fingers.

"We'll be back to pick you up," Jimi said, paying Earl for the gas.

"You sure you want to do this?" Star asked Jimi as they watch the gas dock recede, Earl staring after them in amazement. They'd talked about it before. Since they were leaving the next day, and Earl was cute and would be oh-so-grateful, they figured it was a good time to try.

"It'll be so hot watching you get off," Jimi said, chewing on her ear.

Just the idea got Jimi going. They didn't want to wait until they returned later for Earl, so they let the boat drift as they made love all afternoon. But the idea of a third was hot enough to have them both going again that evening when they picked him up.

"Hi," Star called, as Jimi navigated the boat expertly up to the dock.

"Hi," Earl said, hopping aboard without tying the boat off. "You need gas?"

"We're good to go," Jimi called down, pulling the boat away from the dock.

"Why don't you slip this off," Star suggested, flicking Earl's collar. She and Jimi were already naked.

Earl was clearly uncomfortable, but not so much that he'd miss out on an opportunity to have a woman like Star—and with her husband's encouragement. He shucked his shorts and kicked off his shoes as Star tugged him toward one of the padded benches that surrounded the rear deck.

Taking a seat, Star pulled Earl over to her. He gently kissed her lips and then, with Miss March guiding his head, dropped his lips lower to kiss and suckle her breasts. Jimi watched as he brought the boat into a secluded cove that he had picked for their little ménage. A bit off the beaten path, it afforded a little extra privacy on the vast lake.

By the time Jimi came downstairs, the video camera loaded and in hand, Star was nursing at Earl's hard cock, tickling his balls with her long nails.

"Ah," Earl cried out, his head and upper body jerking forward each time she hit a nerve, which was pretty often.

Jimi stroked himself and shouted encouragement as he filmed.

But as Star fitted Earl with a condom and pulled him on top of her to guide him inside, something in Jimi shifted. No longer was it a hot and erotic scene. It was someone getting ready to fuck his wife.

"No," Jimi said, setting the camera aside and moving toward them. "I don't think so."

And before he could slide into home, Earl was thrown out,

his clothes and shoes tumbling after him into the shallow water of the cove. He was treated to the sound of their laughter and the fumes of the boat's engine as they powered away, leaving him naked and treading water a long way from anyone.

As with all good things, the trip to Lake Havasu came to an end. It was time to return to their lives and to the obligations of the world. Star had promised the *Hy Voltz* people an answer on the script she was supposed to be reading, and on the trip home she actually read the script, or what there was of it. It was really just an overgrown version of what Star had come to understand was called a treatment. Kind of like someone was just telling the idea for the story with a few scenes written out to give the impression.

But the idea was irresistible, and both she and Jimi took to it as she read it to him in the car. It had started as a project that they were in together. His enthusiasm and confidence that she could play the part had been the main reason she'd said yes in the first place. He had even sat with her when she'd made the decision to get the tattoo of cable around her upper arm.

It was something new to do together. They had been virtually inseparable since that night they'd gone to Madre de la Perla in Cabo. In that moment on that May morning, Star stood on the prow of that yacht rolling into the harbor at Cannes like a tsunami engulfing everything in her path.

3

three little birds

The good news was that, due to Star's overwhelming reception at Cannes, *Hy Voltz* was the most hotly anticipated film of the year. The bad news was that, due to Star's overwhelming reception at Cannes, *Hy Voltz* was the most hotly anticipated film of the year.

Star's little summer movie project was rapidly turning into a big-budget action-adventure film, and the quirky little script was being turned into a formula-one, high-performance blockbuster. The original director had been replaced by someone with big-budget-movie credits. So, an untried Star and an untried studio were rushing to supersize the production, trying to keep their original production date so that Star could resume shooting her two television series in the fall.

As preproduction hurtled toward the commencement of principal photography, the only thing higher than the expectations was the tension.

And so it was fortuitous that Theresa had called with her "bad" news.

She and Star had spoken since Cabo and the wedding, but they were taking their time warming back up to each other after a few sharp words over the trip and the wedding and Jimi. Star had wanted to pick up the phone so often, just to vent about some crazy day or other on the *Hy*-way, as she and Jimi had taken to calling it, so, when the call came, Star was glad to hear from her best friend.

"Hello, Star?" Theresa said, her greeting almost a plea.

"Theresa!" Star trumpeted. "Hi! How great. What's up, you sound a little stressed!"

"He fired me! Can you believe that?"

"What?"

"Mother fired me," Theresa said, breaking down again for the umpteenth time since she'd gotten home from her former job at Mother Pearl's. Despite the name on the door, the place belonged to Bernie Weintraub, whom everyone called Mother.

Theresa had paced, cried, eaten all the sweets in the house, and, when that had failed, remembered what she'd done in every crisis since Eddie Greenleaf had kissed her behind the equipment shed in third grade. She called Star.

"I can't believe it," Star said, sitting heavily on the lowest step on the main staircase at the Malibu house. "What happened? Did you two fight?"

"No, he said it was for my own good," Theresa wailed.

"For your own good?"

"Well, I was planning to go to school at Manatee Community this fall," Theresa explained, sniffling but getting the better of her tears for a moment. "They have that accelerated dental assistant's program that I've been thinking about."

"Right," Star said, leaning against the railing to avoid being trampled by a workman who was carrying painting equipment and scaffolding up the stairs, which concerned her, as she hadn't arranged for anything on the second floor to be painted.

"So anyway, Vanda ran off and got married," Theresa said.

"No!" Star gasped. "Not that stripper? Isn't he gay now?"

"That was last month. He switched back after the sugar daddy dumped him, and she wanted to stake a claim before he changed back again," Theresa clarified sadly. "So we're not only shorthanded, but since Vanda took off to follow his dance troupe, I'm senior girl."

"And she was your roommate," Star added, realizing the gravity of the situation.

"Well, that's another problem," Theresa agreed. "So, I decided I'd put off Manatee for the foreseeable future. But you know how Mother is. He said, 'Not this time, young lady. You're fired. Get out of this dump and go to school before you're too old and stupid to learn anything.'" Theresa began crying again. "And then he said, 'You know, Theri, those tits won't last forever.'"

"That's not true," Star said, coming to her defense. "Those implants I got you are top-of-the-line. They'll outlast all of us."

"I know it," Theresa wailed. "He meant I was getting too old."

"No, he didn't, sweetie," Star soothed, knowing that irony was not the only reason that their former employer was called Mother. "He wants you to get out of there and make something of yourself, and he's right."

"But school doesn't start till this fall, and even if I do go, I was counting on the summer tourist season at Mother's to help me afford it."

"Well, Theresa, today may just be your lucky day," Star said, leaping up to avoid a section of scaffolding that came crashing down the stairs after escaping from some unseen source that she searched the upper hall to discover.

It was the perfect plan.

Theresa would come out and work as Star's assistant on the movie. And Star would be able to hang on to her sanity with her fingernails as she shot her first major motion picture, dealt with being a newlywed, and was dissected on the daily news.

Even better, it worked out that Theresa could bring her current boyfriend, JC, along. Jimi was in the market for a trainer, and Juan Carlo was one of Miami's hottest fitness consultants, working with Miami's elite as well as plenty of Hollywood's A-list while they visited their Miami places. Jimi had always thought himself too skinny and was determined to start bulking up that summer, a goal JC assured Jimi was within his grasp in just a few quick sessions.

Star thought Jimi looked fine. The only part of his body that she might conceivably have wanted larger was plenty big enough, and no amount of exercising was ever going to change that.

Jimi and Star were devoted to one another. They were inseparable: eating every meal together, working out together, taking on each and every task as a team. They were enthusiastically wading into redoing the house, shopping together for each plant that was going into making over the grounds of the Malibu house from sand and rocks into a garden worthy of their personal Eden—Jimiville, as Star had taken to calling it. To Star's surprise, Jimi was very knowledgeable about horticulture, knowing the names, often even the Latin ones, of every plant they saw and considered.

He seemed possessed of some magical properties where plants were concerned.

But as Star's career and the work on the film took more and more of her time, Jimi switched his focus, and husband and wife were inseparable, either on the set or in meetings or in preparation for her role as the first female action adventure hero. Since Cannes, their visibility was up and they stuck more closely together than ever.

Because of her own athletic prowess, not to mention her complete moviemaking naïveté, Star decided to do most of her stunt work herself. She began frequenting the firing ranges and became competent with all manner of guns; she found the power arousing. She took martial arts training and boned up on her old gymnastics skills. It was fun and exhilarating to discover that she still had it in her.

One afternoon, after a costume fitting at the soundstages where most of the interiors were to be shot, she ran into the executive producer, Steph, and some of the other more minor executives on the project. "How's it going?" Steph asked in greeting as they passed. In answer, Star did a standing backflip, shook his hand, and went on her way. Their applause accompanied her exit, which she made with a bow.

Jimi helped out where he could.

One of the many stunts that Star had elected to do, at least in part, was to ride a motorcycle. Star felt that since her character rode, learning was a part of understanding her role, and it sounded like fun. The stunt coordinator arranged for her to go to a Westside Harley dealership to take out the kind of bike she would be riding in the film for a test-drive to "get the feel of it." Jimi insisted on accompanying her, but when the time for her lesson arrived, he was delayed by negotiations over a possible new Fools Brigade project.

Figuring it was no big deal, and actually quite delighted by the opportunity, Star kept the appointment. Arriving at the dealership dressed in a pair of cutoffs, a tube top, heels, and a rhinestone-studded necklace that said FOXY in bold block letters, she felt she had mastered the most important part of successful motorcycling: costuming. "What else would a biker chick wear, right?" she said in response to the appreciative whistles she got from her "instructors" at the dealership.

As with most things in her life, it simply never occurred to Star that she couldn't ride a motorcycle. So she did. The instructor explained the basics. Star kicked the bike into life and took the Sportster for a spin.

Jimi roared up to the dealership riding his own bike complete with illegal ape hangers about a half hour after Star's departure, demanding to know where she was. "What the hell do you mean, she already left?" his voice echoed through the tile-and-glass enclosure that housed the brightly colored, chrome-encrusted crotch rockets.

"Well, she seemed to know what she was doing," the salesman shrugged. "She said she just wanted to get the feel of the bike and so we let her go."

"How long ago?" Jimi said, panic beginning to creep into his voice.

"Half an hour? Forty-five minutes?"

"If anything's happened to her, I'll come back here and take you and this whole place apart," Jimi said with such frightening quiet that the salesman stepped back even though Jimi had not advanced on him.

"Look, man . . ." he began, holding his hands up in surrender.

"Which way did she go?"

"Toward the beach." The man paled as he began to realize the possible consequences, with or without Jimi's threats, if anything happened to Star.

Jimi took his bike and zigzagged up and down the streets that radiated from the dealership. Eventually he caught up to Star and fell in beside her. She felt happy and free as they made their way back to the dealership. As they pulled back in, Star popped the clutch and the bike fell on her painfully, burning her leg on the hot engine exhaust pipe.

"Fuck, you made me nervous," Star said to Jimi. "I was doing fine. Fuck!"

Like an overprotective parent's, Jimi's help didn't always make things better.

Making movies is like watching paint dry. You set up for hours, then shoot for a relatively few minutes, then set up some more. And work on a house *is* watching paint dry, and theirs was drying even more slowly than anticipated. The combination was maddening. "You're just trying to do too much, Star," Jimi bellowed, when there was to be yet another delay while the tile people did yet another acid wash to remove the yellowed finish on the tiles in the enormous main hallway and staircase.

"Jimi," Star sighed, trying to make peace while she got ready for her next shot. "We agreed this had to be done, remember? And we can't get back in the house if we can't get in the front door or use the stairs. Try to be patient."

"I'll be patient in my own house," Jimi groused, slouching on the trailer's sofa.

The soundstages where the shoot was to take place were a long way from the beach communities where both their houses were located. Star rented an apartment in the ultrahip area off Sunset Boulevard. The idea was to bring them closer to the set and, she hoped, make it easier on both during the renovation.

Despite the fact that they owned two homes and were renting an apartment, Star and Jimi ended up living in a hotel that was closer to the shoot. It was fun and reminded them of when they'd first met.

Above and beyond the tension of the shoot and the remodeling, the news of the body in Lake Havasu had hit the news. Though no one had thought to link the two, husband and wife were even more on edge—and inseparable. And what with principal photography beginning on the movie, Jimi became still more security conscious, still more protective of Star.

But neither had any experience with moviemaking, so they got off to a rocky start.

The opening of the film was envisioned as a dance sequence in which Star's character performed her acrobatic choreography swinging from a "live" electrical cable suspended above the heads of the crowd in a cross between a postapocalyptic strip club and the Thunderdome. Special effects wizards had labored for days to make it appear that electricity issued from Star's fingertips, showering the audience and her scantily clad body with sparks each time she came in contact with the metal framework surrounding the stage. It was genius. Not only would it capitalize on the film's voluptuous star, it made the point that her character was impervious to, and an excellent conductor of, high voltage, hence her name, Hy Voltz.

Star's costume for the number was little more than an unlaced corset that partially exposed her breasts, a "problem" made worse by all the swinging. She looked amazing and Jimi couldn't resist. They were barricaded in Star's trailer until the director went ballistic.

Steph arrived on the set and explained to Jimi that Star would have to pay hundreds of thousands of dollars for the lost shoot unless they got the shot that day.

And so rather than an eight-hour shoot starting in the morning, it turned out to be an eleven-hour shoot that didn't even get started until eight o'clock at night.

"Hello," Star answered groggily.

"Star?"

"Theresa?" she said, not yet realizing that it was time to return to the set. "What is it? What time—"

"I'm downstairs, are you ready?"

"I'm, um, not yet," Star lied, dragging herself partly out of bed as she tried to act as if she'd been up longer than just the length of their conversation. "Could you come up?"

"JC's with me, do you want us to come up?"

"No, you just wait right there. I'll be down as soon as I'm ready." Star clicked off the phone and threw it in the other direction as she rolled over, snuggled up against Jimi, and went back to sleep.

"Star and Rockstar Boy Toy Turn Movie Set into Mayhem."

"Star Wood Leigh Fined Thousands for Production Delays."

"Jimi Deed's Wild Man Act Overshadows *Hy Voltz* Production."

It didn't take long for the rumors to turn into headlines.

The articles about how difficult Star was to work with began to appear by the end of the first week of shooting. The days and the shoots ran long, and the time she insisted on with Jimi made them longer. Star paid the price. Tired and exhausted trying to please the director, the producers, and Jimi, she was miserable and unhappy with her work.

Finally, almost by accident, Star hit on the solution.

It happened one day about a week into the shoot. Missy, Billy, Skip, and Theresa were buzzing around the trailer. Jimi and JC were just outside on the workout equipment the studio had provided for her to keep in shape during the demanding shoot. Jimi's workout schedule was showing remarkable results, and JC's reputation in Hollywood was growing as well.

Star was back for a costume change and touch-up on her makeup and had just begun the arduous process of getting out of her costume. It was no small achievement, given that just her lace-up gloves took about twenty minutes to put on. The series of corsets that comprised her costumes were even more tedious and time-consuming to remove, even more so since they had learned the hard way that due to Star's low blood pressure, if they unlaced her too quickly, she fainted.

"I just don't get it," Billy said, exasperated with a knot in the laces of Star's glove. "How the hell are superheroes supposed to do all the amazing stuff they do in these impossible outfits?"

"Really," Skip agreed, ruminatively combing out Star's hair. "Can you imagine having a huge fight with half a dozen bad guys wearing a cape? How could that possibly help?"

"Or chase villains in these shoes?" Missy agreed, wrestling off one of Star's stiletto-heeled, thigh-high, black-leather, lace-up boots.

"Or outsmart the evil geniuses with this updo," Star added, laughing along. " 'Cause you know . . ." she only had to begin.

"I can hardly think with all this hair," everyone chimed in.

"Where's the party?" Jimi said, coming into the trailer just as Star was coming out of the outfit. "You boys had better be gay, in here with my wife's tits hanging out."

"We could prove it to you," Skip said from under a wickedly arched brow.

"No, that won't be necessary," Jimi said, holding up both hands in surrender. "I'll take your word for it."

"Where's the fun in that?" Billy said, tapping his chin with the rubber tip of a prop knife that he'd taken from the sheath in Star's glove.

There was a knock at the door.

"Miss Leigh? Five minutes."

"My wife's fucking name is Deed," Jimi shouted in reply. "And it's gonna take longer than five minutes. Could everyone excuse us?"

"Great," Skip said, taking a seat on the workout bench. "Go tell your masters," he said nastily to the production assistant. The kid ran off.

"And could you bring back some lattes?" Billy called after him.

Jimi and Star began trashing the inside of the trailer—their third since the shoot had begun.

Jimi buried his face in her breasts, tweaking one and then the other nipple with his teeth as she tore at his clothes. They collapsed onto the floor, still clutching each other; Star shoved his Levi's down with her feet, her legs wrapped around him. And then he was inside her, and he began slamming Star around the trailer as the two took their tension out on each other. It was like the rough sex they both liked—biting, clawing, and slam-fucking each other against the walls, on all the furniture, and finally against the door of the trailer.

She caught his lip between her teeth and actually drew blood as he pinned her against the frail metal door and drove himself into her with all his force in each impassioned thrust. Rather than catching a rhythm, he would pull himself almost all the way out and then throw himself against her to find new depths to her and her passion.

The little group just outside silently regarded the door straining at its hinges.

"You think it's gonna blow?" Theresa asked mischievously.

"Should we do something?" Missy wondered aloud, unable to look away. "I mean, do you think they're all right?"

"Are you kidding?" Billy laughed.

"I wouldn't mind doing that," Skip snorted.

"I wouldn't mind it if you *could* do that," Billy said, laughing harder.

"I wonder if we can get the trailer next," JC said, grinning, taking Theresa's hand.

"Is everything okay?" Steph inquired, approaching the trailer warily.

"Oh, God!" Star's scream rang out from inside the trailer, accompanied by their violent pounding against the door.

"Should we do something?"

"You got a cigarette they can bum afterwards?" Skip asked with a knowing smile.

"Fuck yeah," Jimi shouted, loud enough to be heard back inside the soundstage. "Baby, baby . . . all . . . fuck!"

"Oh," Steph said. "I heard there was trouble. When do you think they'll be done?"

"That sounded like the end to me," Billy said, trying not to laugh.

"Well, I mean . . . ," Steph began.

"Come on, JC," Jimi said, emerging from the trailer. "Let's go get some supplies for tonight." He stumbled out of the trailer, smiling at everyone, climbed into his Testarossa, lit a cigarette, and left.

"Shit," Star said, walking out the door of the trailer. "I'll need an hour-and-a-half shower."

"Got it," Steph said, departing.

It was so simple.

Star had a new secret weapon. Well, it wasn't that new, but she had a new strategy for using it.

The real challenge became keeping Jimi happy and her hair, makeup, and costumes intact for the next scene. Star joked she was going to write a book of "safe" sex tips—positions to maximize pleasure while preserving hair and makeup. It was a strange peace and there were still delays, to keep the production consistently and very publicly a week behind schedule. But it kept everyone happy at least, but wary of the next delay as the production moved forward.

And so it was, with everyone lulled into a false sense of security, that the fateful day arrived.

Star was really thin and exhausted and kept going fueled on adrenaline and coffee. Jimi was there at her side all the time, but that only meant their sex life was vigorous and more active. Star didn't mind so much, except that she was trying to make a movie.

The day that everything changed was a particularly physically challenging one for Star. She was doing most of her stunt work. The day's stunt was one that might well have been given over to the professionals. It was a judgment call, but whatever the verdict, it was the most strenuous stunt work Star had done to that point on the shoot.

The shot called for Star, captured by the movie's villains, to be hung upside down and hoisted several stories into the air to participate in a fistfight with men on an elevated catwalk.

"And wearing a rubber bodice, high heels, and enough hair spray to hold up a Dolly Parton tour," Skip said, shaking his head in disapproval as he helped her get ready. "It's too much. Your stunt people should be doing this."

"It ain't fittin'. It just ain't fittin'," Billy said in his best Hattie McDaniel.

"Fiddle-dee-dee," Star said, sawing the air with an imaginary fan.

"It ain't fittin'."

"Star, you okay to do this, babe?" Jimi asked, distracted. "I'm good if you're good, but if not . . ."

"No, I'm fine," Star said, pleased by his show of interest, but not wanting to risk shutting down the production. "It'll be fine."

"Okay, then," Jimi said, edging toward the door. "It's just, well, JC and I need to go get some cigarettes."

"You boys run on," she said, knowing that his absence would speed up what was already promising to be a long day.

"Cool," he said, leaning in and smearing her makeup with a substantive good-bye kiss. "Sorry Billy," he added sheepishly when he saw what he'd done.

"Well, that move's not going in the book," Billy snorted, only slightly amused.

Heading out the door, Jimi closed it behind him.

All anyone knew that day was that Jimi had left the set and Star was ready on time and the shoot began on schedule. Skip hid his eyes as Star was strapped onto the steel beam and hoisted high above the studio floor. Once she achieved the desired height, a trapeze swing was lowered from the ceiling so that Star could sit upright between setups until they needed her. It was somewhat more comfortable, but not a lot, and it required Star to swing backward, grab the ropes, and hoist herself onto the bar, where she sat with her legs more or less straight in front of her, still lashed to the I beam for the sequence.

It was hideous.

And it was the only comfort available to her in a long, long day of shooting. She'd slip off the swing, they'd get a couple of shots of her fighting, swinging, and hanging upside down as she met the enemy on the steel catwalk across from her. Then she'd perch on the steel bar of the trapeze swing and sip lukewarm coffee through a straw. And then they'd film a bit more.

Finally, she was finding a use for the gymnastics training she'd had from the time she was nine years old.

It was getting done, but it was difficult and exhausting.

They had been at it for several hours when, in the middle of one of the fight sequences, Star began screaming and writhing, taking out two of her opponents and almost knocking a third off the catwalk.

There was a moment of uncertainty. It was a fight sequence and it seemed that Star might either be out of control or trying to dial up the action.

Skip's lips disappeared and his mouth became a line between his nose and his jaw as he watched the action and tried to keep quiet. Billy squeezed his hand.

"Cut," the director called. It had looked great and he was glad they'd gotten it, but it wasn't on the storyboards, so he wasn't even sure they could use it. "That was amazing, Star, but save your energy. Let's try it again, from one, and just the movements we've discussed."

Star hung limply from the I beam.

"Star?" the director called through the bullhorn he was using to direct the sequence. "You ready?"

No response.

"I think she's out," one of the players called down from the catwalk.

"Oh, God," Skip said, leaping to his feet. "Get her down from there now."

The crew, uncertain, were slow to react, as Skip, not the director, had issued the directive.

"Cut her down, cut her down, cut her fucking down," Skip began screaming, near hysteria when no one responded to his earlier plea.

Billy rushed out to her and caught her in his arms as she was lowered from the ceiling. The grips began untying the lashings that held her ankles to the I beam, but Skip grabbed a box cutter and slashed through the bindings and safety straps.

Once she was freed, Billy and others carried her to the trailer, where they laid her out on the sofa.

Missy rubbed Star's wrists with ice as Billy checked her head for blood.

A number of the crew and some of the cast gathered outside Star's trailer door to find out what was going on. Theresa tried to reach Jimi. As it was, she only got both his and JC's voice mail.

Initially, it was thought that Star had hit her head on the railing and knocked herself out, but there was no bump or blood or other obvious sign. Star moaned as she slipped marginally into consciousness. "Mom?" she groaned. "I didn't start it, I swear."

Slowly, Missy began to unlace the rubber bodice, and Star sat up, screamed out in pain, and passed out again.

"What is going on?" Skip demanded, rising and storming to the door. "Where is an ambulance?"

"It's complicated," the shop steward said with a shrug.

"No, it isn't," Skip said. "It's 911. How hard is that?"

"Well, the insurance guys are unclear on whose responsibility it is," Steph explained, covering the mouthpiece of his cell.

"Are you kidding me with that?" Skip snorted. "Well, I'm not sure that it makes any difference whose fucking responsibility—"

There was familiar tire-squealing in the near distance, and a hush fell over the group.

"Thank God," Skip said, folding his arms.

Jimi drove the car up to the trailer at full speed, knocking over a catering table and some lighting equipment that had been in his way. Without a word he leaped from the car, stormed into the trailer, swept Star into his arms, and carried her out where JC helped him get her into the tiny sports car.

The first of three ambulances arrived just as Jimi was pulling away; two followed the car to the hospital, carrying friends and crew, as did the insurance van.

As always, Jimi's reaction was unexpected. Suddenly serious and quiet, he pumped the doctors for information, was at Star's side as much as they would allow him, and even sometimes when they wouldn't. When he wasn't at her side, he was just outside whatever door she was behind, sitting on the floor if no chair was available. And then only when he was too tired to pace.

"You really do love her, don't you," Billy said, arriving with an order from Starbucks to fuel the little group huddled in the waiting area.

"Dude," Jimi said, a couple of tears escaping in a puff of

what might have been a laugh, "what would you do if it was Skip?"

Billy was so touched and overwrought that he hugged Jimi.

"That may be the nicest thing you've ever said to me," Billy snuffled, breaking the hug abruptly and getting back to the coffee.

"Don't let it get around," Jimi said quietly, glad of the comfort. He was truly worried about Star. And he felt guilty for not being there when she'd needed him.

"Mr. Deed?" the doctor said, emerging from the room. "She's awake and she's asking for you."

Without a word Jimi rushed past the doctor and into the room. Kneeling beside the bed, he put his arms around Star, more or less lying across her and the bed.

"Jimi," she said quietly, stroking his hair. "Get off of me, you're hurting me, babe."

"Oh, sorry," he said, sitting up, afraid to touch her at all.

She took his hand and kissed it.

"As long as you two are here," the doctor said, closing the door and following Jimi into the room, "I've got some news about Mrs. Deed's condition."

"So, what's up, Doc?" Star asked with a little giggle, unable to resist the line.

"Is it serious?" Jimi said, the color draining from his face, feeling as though he might fall.

"Well, yes," the doctor said evenly. "Star had an ovarian cyst about the size of a grapefruit, which burst. There was a loss of blood and drop in blood pressure."

"And a lot of pain," Star put in.

"Yes, and everything looks good," the doctor went on.

"The bleeding is stopped and we're running some tests, but we're optimistic. We'll take care of the surgical correction through the belly button, and she should be up and around soon."

"Oh, that's great, Doc," Jimi said, shifting nervously from one foot to the other.

Star only sighed, too tired for much more.

"The bad news is, you miscarried," the doctor concluded solemnly.

"Miscarried?" Jimi repeated, disbelieving.

"You mean I was—" Star's tears cut her off.

"Pregnant." The doctor nodded. "But not for very long."

Jimi held Star until she fell asleep, the realization of what they'd lost hitting them again and again.

4

once upon a time

 Inquiries from the film's producers about Star's return to the set arrived at the hospital within hours. She was too stunned to reply.

As soon as the doctors gave Star the all clear, Jimi sneaked her out the back door of the hospital with the laundry and into Star's Range Rover. Jimi had arranged for Theresa and JC to park the room-sized ride by the loading dock, thinking it would be more comfortable for Star than his cramped sports coupe. JC brought Jimi's car around to the front door of the hospital, and the press cued up to capture the moment. The ploy was pretty successful and they thought they were home free as they made their way to hide out at their unfinished beachfront home.

They didn't talk much. Jimi didn't know what to say and Star was too tired to speak. She took his hand as he drove toward home down the familiar stretch of Pacific Coast Highway, PCH as it's better known to the locals, wedged between the beach on one side and the sheer rock face of the mountains into which the road was carved.

"Thanks for getting me out of there," she sighed, curling up in her seat.

"Nothing to it," he said, raising her hand to his lips and kissing it gently. "I'm just glad you're okay."

A dark Ford Explorer darted in front of them without warning, and Jimi swerved, nearly plastering their car into the man-made cliff that ran along the shoulder, before rebounding back onto the highway. He flipped off the driver just in time to get his picture taken by the paparazzi inside.

The Explorer played a dangerous game of cat and mouse with the Range Rover in the four lanes of busy traffic on a winding and unforgiving roadway that offered little margin for error. Jimi tried to outrun the carload of paparazzi, but they caught up and cut them off again and again.

Star was screaming and crying, overwrought from an emotional day and the terror of the chase. Jimi too was screaming and overwrought, but his emotions took a more violent turn as he shouted profanities and picked up the speed of the chase.

Finally, patience ran out. On his last pass to gain the lead, he cut in front of the photographers' car, forcing them off the road, where they hit a parked car and the stone cliff wall before crumpling to a rest. Just as quickly, Jimi had stopped the Range Rover and was running toward them with a tire iron in his hand, Star close behind. The stalkers, unable to get their car restarted, rolled up their windows and locked their doors as they braced for attack.

Star began trying to kick in the driver's door as Jimi began smashing every piece of glass on the car—the headlights, the mirror, the taillights.

"We love you, Star!" the car's occupants screamed in their defense.

"Fuck you, you assholes!" she shouted in her blind rage. "You almost killed us. Fuck you!"

As the windshield shattered into a spiderweb of broken glass, the car's occupants' dog jumped up on the dashboard and began barking in loyal defense of his indefensible masters.

"Jimi, stop, there's a dog!" Star screamed, leaping back from the car where she had been trying to break the driver's window.

It was an act of will, and he took a couple of swipes, denting the car's hood, before he gave it up entirely, but Jimi let it go. Together the two raced away, frightened more by their own rage than by the accident.

Afraid of retaliation for the incident and on the run from the relentless film producers, they returned briefly to the hotel in Pasadena to get a few things and plan a getaway.

But it was not to be.

Still shaken from the experience on PCH, they headed for the hotel bar to get a drink to settle their nerves. One quiet drink was all they managed.

Jimi's cell rang.

"It's JC," he said, checking the phone. "I'm going to take this one and find out what's going on."

"Okay, I'm going to the ladies'," Star said. Sliding out of

the booth where they had enjoyed a fleeting moment of privacy, she knocked her purse on the ground and leaned over to pick it up.

"Nice ass," said a guy sitting with his family at a nearby table.

"What did you say?" Jimi said, standing suddenly at the man's table, almost before it seemed possible.

"What?" The guy looked up, startled by Jimi's appearance out of nowhere.

"What did you say to my wife?" Jimi demanded, raking everything off the man's table, covering everyone there with fresh guacamole dip—the house specialty.

"Take it easy," the guy said, standing and leaping back from the flying debris.

There were screams as other people fled the bar.

"Jimi, let it go, it doesn't matter to me," Star said quietly, taking his arm.

"It matters to me." Jimi shook her off. "That's my wife, you stupid motherfucker. Apologize."

"You want *me* to apologize?" the man asked in amazement.

And Jimi, cell phone still in his hand from the conversation he'd been having when it had all started, decked the guy, dislocating two fingers, knocking the guy unconscious, and disconnecting the call.

The *Tits* was a 152-foot yacht belonging to zillionaire concert promoter turned record executive Missouri Harris, MO to his friends. He'd made a fortune developing trendy record labels and then unloading them at the top of the market onto slow-moving corporate media behemoths just before the trend went bust.

It was just the sort of yacht you'd expect a rock promoter to have. Mirrored ceilings, marble Jacuzzis, and leopard-skin everything, it made the merely vulgar seem commonplace. It also made for the perfect hiding place for Star and Jimi. On the run from angry paparazzi, the producers, and the authorities, their business and their pictures plastered on the covers of everything in print in most languages around the world, the middle of the Pacific Ocean was just about the only place left where they still might find a little peace. Even then, it was not a sure thing. But at least when the time came, they would see them coming.

So, it was a good thing that Jimi was one of the intimates who called Mr. Harris MO. The two had worked together early in Jimi's career when MO had produced the *Hell in a Handbasket* tour when Fools Brigade had opened for the Prince of Darkness himself, Sidney Melbourne. Jimi, Sid, and MO had gotten into so many scrapes with the authorities during the first leg of the tour that MO sent Fools Brigade into the studio to record a new album he financed.

It not only resulted in a platinum album, it was the beginning of a lifelong friendship that was their lifesaver that Fourth of July weekend.

Besieged in their hotel, Jimi and Star emerged in hoodies, hats, and dark glasses, dove into a waiting limo, and led the paparazzi on merry chase through Old Town before revealing in the parking lot at Huntington Gardens that they were in fact Theresa and JC. The stunt almost got Theresa fired from the production, but covered Jimi and Star's escape.

By the time the ruse was revealed, Jimi and Star were on a

motor launch taking them out for a little much-needed R&R on the borrowed over-the-top yacht. Star was unaware of their destination, and Jimi insisted that she wear a blindfold until the *Tits* was in sight.

"You bought me a boat? It's huge," Star squealed as they drew closer to the three-story behemoth sitting placidly on choppy waters, too big and heavy to be jostled by the roiling water.

"Star," Jimi chided shyly, "you don't have to keep telling me."

She splashed him with water from over the side, and the two were soaked by the time they boarded.

"Let's get out of these wet things," Jimi said, kicking off his shoes and pulling his collared shirt, still buttoned, over his head.

Star joined in, and to the surprise of the astonished crew, the two shucked their clothes in a spirited game of chase. It wasn't anything the crew of the wild party yacht hadn't seen before, they just didn't usually see it so soon. Heedless of the staff, their romp wound them up naked and sprawled on a couple of the sumptuous chaises on the top-level sundeck.

"Um, yes, excuse me, sir," the chief attendant said, politely averting his eyes. "The captain would like to know your pleasure, and I wonder if I might offer any refreshment?"

"Tell the captain we don't want to see land or another boat for a week," Jimi shouted joyously. "And we need champagne right away."

"Very good, sir," the attendant said with a small bow. "I'm Albere, if you need anything; pick up any phone you see. Otherwise, the crew will stay in quarters to afford you your privacy."

"Perfect," Star said, wallowing in the faux-leopard-skin cushions. "This fur had better be fake."

"Absolutely," Jimi replied—hoping.

The world searched frantically for them over the next five days, but Star and Jimi stayed out of sight, wandering the polished mahogany decks nude—or nearly—eating when they felt like it, feasting on caviar, lobsters, and crab washed down with buckets of champagne and making love every time the mood struck them.

As always, their time on the run gave them the chance to remember that they always had each other, and that anything was possible.

Jimi was looking for more sunscreen when he happened on the video camera that had haphazardly been tossed into their luggage when they'd scrambled to escape from their hotel room.

"Smile," he said, waking Star from her nap as she sunbathed nude on the deck off the master cabin. "I love you, babe."

"Jimi," Star moaned. "What's up?"

"I just love you, you complaining?"

"Never." She laughed, taking "little Jimi" in hand, bringing him to full attention, then swallowing him whole.

Jimi fell back onto one of the fur-covered chaises as Star climbed on top of him, her head bobbing in and out of the increasingly erratic shot.

"Here, my turn," he said, lacing his fingers into her hair and pulling her up for air as he handed her the camera.

She howled like a savage, tossing her feet into the air as he began crawling menacingly over her body, his face moving closer and closer to the lens. He growled seductively, then swept her into the air. He plunged himself inside her as he carried her across the deck, bringing her to rest on the marble surface of the outdoor edition of the room's three bars. Glassware and bottles tumbled everywhere as he began to sprint into the home stretch.

Jimi took the camera and zoomed in with a porn aficionado's eye and a surgeon's anatomical expertise to capture in detail their most intimate contact as they joined as one again and again. It was a strange and heady experience for him as he had the feeling he was appearing in the porno and watching it at the same time.

For her part Star was too lost in the actual reality of the moment to be worried about the virtual one. She felt great for a change and was reveling in being fully present in the moment as Jimi's video-enhanced excitement translated into a focus and intensity that took Star along for the ride. She writhed on the cool marble surface, enjoying the feel of her own body as she dragged her hands over her own skin, relishing each little touch.

The sight of Star playing with her own breasts and nipples along with the sight of his own cock pistoning in and out, kicked Jimi's pornographic VR experience up a notch and incited a riot of feeling that played havoc over his body. His excitement only drove him on, and they shouted out endearments as they destroyed the bar and reached the end of their private show. Jimi fell back, exhausted and drained by the moment, their third so far that day, still looking through the lens of the camera he seemed to have forgotten he still had glued to his face.

"That was a-fucking-mazing, babe!" he howled at that cloudless blue sky above them.

"Yeah, baby, it was great," she said, dragging herself off the bar and onto the chaise beside him. "Only, promise me something."

"Anything," he said, sitting up and framing her face in the viewfinder.

"No more camera," she said, reaching out and switching it off.

Paradise and the *Tits* were lost all too soon.

As they were anchored just south of Catalina and surprisingly close to the world that clamored for them, a small fishing boat drew inconspicuously near. Star was swimming nude in the water, and Jimi was, despite their agreement, getting just a few more shots. He'd stopped filming their lovemaking, but he couldn't resist the shots of her perfect, tanned skin flashing at the surface of the warm, choppy water from which he himself had only just emerged. What he didn't know was that Star had sneaked shots of his skinny-dipping before she'd jumped in to join him.

The fishing boat was one of many that had lazily drifted by on that perfect July afternoon. They paid no more attention to it than they had to those earlier. No one knew that Star and Jimi were on board, let alone drifting off the coast of Catalina. Star was still in the water when the smaller boat was put over the side of the fishing vessel and the occupants rowed themselves toward the gangway from which Star and Jimi had been diving.

"Hey," the tanned and weather-beaten man called from under his wide-brimmed hat.

"What's up?" Jimi called genially.

"Just a delivery" came the reply from under the hat.

For her part, Star continued discreetly treading the water, as it was the only thing she was wearing. Jimi left his towel draped around his shoulders, more curious than concerned about their visitors.

As the rowboat reached the gangway, the man removed his hat respectfully and bowed his head in greeting.

"Jimi Deed?" he asked politely.

"Yep," Jimi answered warily.

"For you." The man extended his hand and pushed a long manila envelope toward Jimi.

Clearly this was just the messenger. Jimi figured rightly that the boat and its crew would likely earn more for finding them and delivering the mysterious envelope than they would in a whole week of good fishing.

"Thanks," Jimi said, taking the envelope.

The man tipped his hat politely and, his job happily completed, rowed away with his silent companions.

Jimi regarded the unopened and unmarked envelope for a moment.

"What is it?" Star asked, swimming nearer.

"We may already have won ten million dollars," Jimi said, laughing.

"Don't open it," she said, hoisting herself onto the little, white, expanded metal landing just above the water level at the base of the gangway.

"I don't supposed I really have to," he said, smiling at her sadly.

"No, I guess not," Star said, leaning over and kissing him gently. "Thanks for doing this. I really needed it."

"I'll tell the captain to head for home," he said, drawing her body against his and holding her just a moment more.

It was just as well that they didn't open the envelope. It contained legal documents and prefiling papers along with a letter, which more clearly stated the threat to sue Star for $100 million if she did not return to the set forthwith and recommence shooting.

They took their time getting back up the coast and didn't call until they got back to port in Los Angeles. Star had had the break she needed, and she knew full well that the studio would rather have her finish their film than enjoin them in their threatened lawsuit, so everyone made nice on her return. The trailer was filled with flowers and greetings and notes of sympathy.

JC and Theresa were there to meet them.

For Star, the excitement of making a movie was completely gone, squeezed out of her. Only a shapeless and empty film remained. All that was left was showing up at dawn, trying to get enough footage in the can to cut together into a movie before they ran out of time and money. It left a bad taste in her mouth.

Worse still, the shooting schedules for *Lifeguards* and *Hammer Time* had begun, and so her production schedule became impossibly difficult. Star's final two weeks on *Hy Voltz* took three as she started work on the two television shows.

She enjoyed seeing her friends and put up with what she had to, to get the movie done. After the heartless response to her illness, she didn't really care anymore, letting Jimi take control.

Jimi worked with the producer to make sure Star got enough rest and breaks. They worked to accommodate their Star, who, for her part, had little idea that any of it was even going on. It just seemed to her that despite their being more pressed for time, she had more time to do things like eat or take an afternoon nap or just spend time with Jimi.

By the time the shoot was finished, there were no new friends; only the people Star had been close to before the production, like Billy, Skip, and Missy, was she close to afterward. The producers, the director, and the principals never worked with her again. In fact, after the wrap party on the last day of shooting, they only ever saw one another once—at the premiere.

Her movie career had begun with more promise and fanfare than *Gone with the Wind,* and it ended, at least for the time being, almost unnoticed by any, save those who were merely relieved to be done.

"Not with a bang but a whimper," she said to Jimi as they removed the last of their personal stuff from the trailer to return to their still-unfinished home.

"So this is the way the world ends." Jimi smirked. "I thought there would be more, you know, smoke."

She kissed him for knowing the poem, and the tires of the Testarossa squealed out of that particular parking lot for the last time. "Let's get the fuck out of here. I hope I never make another movie."

5

wild horses

"Which script is it gonna be today?" Stan Merman asked, holding up two scripts as he entered Star's trailer. "Romance or just friends? We can't do it if he's here, but if she doesn't get a little action soon, her fans are going to desert us." He threw himself on the sofa in disgust.

"Well, you've got yourself on the horns of quite the little dilemma there, Stan," Skip said, looking up from his copy of *Variety* with a wicked smile. "I was just reading that you're the executive producer on the number one syndicated television show in the world. You don't seem all that powerful to me."

"Is he coming today or not?" Stan sighed.

The trouble had begun almost as soon as shooting ended

on *Hy Voltz*. Jimi had moved into Star's trailer on the *Lifeguards* lot, and nothing had ever been the same. He'd been a minor disruption the year before when he was flirting with Star, but now that she was Mrs. Deed, he had taken up residence.

So, despite Stan's success, he still got butterflies each day on his way to work as he wondered whether Jimi would be waiting for him.

Star's romance with costar Rufus Forrest was common knowledge. And her romance with costar Antony Cravatta to those who had been able to read for more than two years. Jimi fell into both categories, which meant he'd forbidden Star to be alone in a scene with either man.

Now, Jimi had no actual authority to forbid anything. But Jimi had never had any difficulty getting exactly what he wanted. The set of *Hy Voltz* had taught him how to manage on set and the producers on *Lifeguards* were no match.

For openers, the show filmed outside, so disrupting the shoot was child's play. An afternoon of cutting wheelies in the parking lot with his Ferrari could virtually bring production to a halt. Not to mention throwing a party, cranking up the music, renting a helicopter, inviting over a motorcycle gang for a beer bust, or just simply refusing to allow anyone access to his wife.

In a matter of weeks, both Star's exes had become strangers and were rarely even scheduled to shoot on days when Star was on the set. Ruf was actually kind of pleased about the situation. He was still smarting from Star's unceremonious wedding to the unruly rock star, whose constant presence was a painful reminder of the love he'd lost. For his part, Ant kept count of his pages, and so long as the producers met his arbitrary quota of screen time, he hardly noticed anything else that happened on the show, let alone after "cut" was called.

The only problem was the fans. Star's character, BeeGee, was the show's most popular, and the viewers made it more than clear that they were interested in whomever BeeGee was interested in. Stan didn't really care what the fans wanted, but he cared what the syndicators who bought and sold the show thought, and they only cared what the fans wanted, since audience, not art nor on-set acrimony, was their solitary concern.

That made it Stan's problem.

His solution: Operation Swedish Meatball. Named by Skip and Billy for the show's newest cast member, Sven Erickson, the unpleasant nickname was the kindest part of the covert operation. It began with a disinformation campaign to convince Jimi that Sven was gay. He wasn't, but Jimi was all but oblivious to having Skip and Billy as intimates in Star's life, hence Stan's twisted plan. To that end, step two involved convincing Skip and Billy, for huge concessions, to become confederates in making Jimi, and to some degree Star, believe that Sven was just one of the girls. The final and most complicated component of the ludicrous top-secret scheme was crafting two different scripts for the show, one that included increasingly romantic moments for Star and Sven, and a second that gave no hint there was anything going on.

Jimi was only ever allowed to see the sanitized scripts, and the romance was shot only when he was not expected on the set. So Operation Swedish Meatball remained largely untested. The trouble was, no one ever knew for certain when Jimi was going to be on the set.

"He's not coming," Missy said, laying out the makeup. She was an unindicted coconspirator in Operation Swedish Meatball. She understood the problem, but wasn't crazy about the level of deception necessary.

"How do you know?" Stan asked, hopeful for the first time that morning.

"Well, you did not hear it from me," Missy sighed, debating her truest loyalty to Star and then deciding the best course. "He's supposed to be meeting with someone from a new label and a couple of guys from the band about possibly a new project."

"God, who's the patron saint of musicians?" Stan sighed, leaning forward in an unspoken prayer that Jimi would have to go away on tour. "We need to make an offering or get a medal or whatever it is you do with saints to get them on your side."

"Your support is touching," Skip said with a smirk. "Perhaps you want the patron saint of cynical aspiration."

"I'd perform a tribal war dance at the start of each take if I thought it would help," Stan declared.

"You'd do what?" Star asked, puzzled by Stan's odd behavior.

"Just a figure of speech," Stan said, happily handing her the romance script. "I gotta go talk to Sven. See you on the set."

"What was all that about?" Star asked the little group waiting for her.

"Maybe he got religion." Billy shrugged, taking her bag and leading her to the chair. "You ready to get started or do you need a minute?"

"No, I'm good to go," Star said, shedding the habitual

sweatshirt jacket and falling into the chair. "I'm already exhausted and I haven't even started working yet."

"Want a mocha?" Billy asked, patting the large and largely
unused heap of brass and copper fittings. "I think I've figured
out how to use this thing."

"Billy, no one wants another incident," Skip warned, sam-
pling Star's hair tentatively, contemplating the next steps.

"Yeah, someone could really get hurt," Missy agreed, popping some moist towels into the microwave. "That milk gets
pretty hot, not to mention the steam."

"Plus, remember that thing we saw on the news about
that coffee bar in Sherman Oaks?" Skip said, shaking a warning comb in Billy's direction. "The whole thing could just
blow."

"I saw that," Missy said, programming the machine.
"They found pieces of the roof in Tarzana."

"You should probably just wait until Jimi gets here," Star
agreed, remembering how long it had taken to get the choco-
late syrup out of everything in the trailer the last time Billy
had tried to operate the espresso machine.

End of conversation.

"Jimi's coming?" Missy said, looking up from the spinning
towels and then realizing and feeling instantly guilty. "I
thought he had the meeting with the record people."

"It wasn't a real label," Star said sadly. "It turned out to be
one of those infomercial compilation deals. So it really didn't
involve the band. The agent went."

"Oh," Missy said, ignoring the reminder bell on the microwave as she stared out the door after Stan. "Well."

"Are you okay, Missy?" Star asked, puzzled by her curious
behavior.

"She was dropped on her head as a child," Skip whispered into Star's ear. "Let's get started."

Hair and makeup for *Lifeguards* was mostly about upkeep and maintenance. Skip got her hair up a bit and Billy got the pink lips, lashes, and eyeliner on her. The rest of the time the three took turns freshening her up as the sand, wind, and water destroyed their work, though it mostly fell to Missy.

Jimi came in just as Star was getting ready to go over the day's pages.

"Hey, babe," he said, leaning down to kiss her on the top of the head. "What's up?"

"Hey, sweetie," Star said, reaching up to stroke his face as she leafed through the pages. "How was your morning?"

"Kinda boring," he said, stuffing his hands in his pockets. "Waited for the tile guy. Met up with some of my boys, but they had stuff. Thought I could hang with you," he suggested, taking a chair next to her.

Missy and Skip moved nearer the door.

"I'll tell you what you can do," Billy said, taking his hand and dragging him away. "You can teach me to work this coffee machine. You're the only one anyone trusts to work it, and sometimes I want espresso when you're not here."

"Billy, my man," Jimi said, in his element, "there's nothing to it."

By the time everyone had their favorite, the tension had dissolved. Star looked over the day's pages while Missy worrid how to let Stan know the pages weren't safe or get Jimi to leave. "So what are you up to this afternoon?" Star asked, sipping her mocha.

"Nada," he said, taking his espresso straight with a twist

of lemon. "Thought I'd just hang. What are you shooting today?"

"Some dialogue scenes at the lifeguard stand with Sven," Star said.

"Oh, Sthven," Jimi lisped, making a joke of it with Skip and Billy.

They laughed nervously.

"What's that about?" Star asked, thinking she was cautioning Jimi about making fun of Skip and Billy.

"Just a little joke between me and your boys," Jimi chuckled with Skip and Billy.

"Really?" Star asked, eyebrows raised. "What's the joke?"

"Guy stuff," Skip said, wrinkling his nose dismissively.

"Yeah, guy stuff," Billy echoed.

"Guy stuff?" Star asked incredulously. "That the three of *you* have in common?"

"Yep," Jimi said smugly.

Before the conversation could progress any further, Stan arrived with Sven and the episode's director. "Star, are you . . . Oh," he trailed off. "Jimi. Hi. You're . . . here."

"Yeah, thought I'd come by, check in," Jimi said, giving Stan an intentionally complicated handshake just for the fun of making him look uncool. "Sven, you and Star are at bat today. Your hair looks really nice."

"Thanks." Sven was always a bit put off by Jimi's manner toward him, but unable to put his finger on just why. He turned to check his hair in the mirror.

Jimi swapped a look with Skip, rolling his eyes behind Sven's back as he primped.

Skip let a snort of laughter escape.

"Well, it looks like you're busy," Stan said, shoving the director back through the door. "Come on, Sven, we'll come back—"

"Stick around," Jimi said, putting his arm around Sven's waist and guiding him chivalrously into a chair. "We were using the new espresso maker you got for the trailer, Stan. Billy makes a really mean latte. What'll you have?"

"That'd be great," Sven said, a little flustered by Jimi's familiarity, but taking it as a sign of generosity. He was new to the show and so had no experience of Jimi. "That'd give us a chance to talk before we start shooting."

"Well, I've got to get back to the set," the director said, rushing for the door.

"I'd better go with you," Stan said, following hurriedly.

"No, wait, guys," Sven called after them. "They're in the middle of setup and they'll come for you as soon as they're ready. They know where we are. I'd really like the chance to go over this before we shoot it."

"I'm not thinking we're going to have time," the director said evasively.

"Yeah, we're running way behind," Stan agreed, again pushing for the door.

"What?" Sven asked, completely confused. "But the whole reason we came over here—"

"Was to let Star know that we wouldn't have time for the scene today," the director said, riding over him.

"So we're not going to get the chance to do the make-out scene?"

Icy silence.

Stan and the director, their backs to the room, froze in the doorway.

Skip examined his copy of *Variety* very closely as Billy bus-
ied himself with the lattes.

The only sound was of steam escaping as Billy heated the
milk.

"Don't worry, Sven," Jimi said, breaking the silence and
patting him on the shoulder. "It's just like kissing a guy."

Even the sound of escaping steam stopped.

"Well, I mean, I know it's impersonal, but that's just the
point," Sven said. Completely misinterpreting Jimi's mean-
ing, Sven rose and spoke to the director, who was forced to
turn back. "I'd like to take the time to do what we can to
bring some life into it. It's the first time for these two characters, it's a little unmotivated, and I think it's important."

Still no one spoke.

"Well, Star always says that she just imagines that she's
kissing her husband," Jimi added, trying to be helpful. "You
just do the same."

"That's absolutely right, Jimi," Stan said triumphantly,
turning back into the room, as Operation Swedish Meatball
succeeded beyond his wildest dreams. "Good advice. Don't
you think, Brock?" He gave the director an elbow.

"Right," Brock said. "Just pretend you're kissing your
husband. Transference is a powerful way to bring, um, reality
to a situation when there's, uh, no time for preparation."

"Transference, that's the ticket," Jimi said, passing Sven
the latte from Billy's inert hand and giving him an affectionate
little pat on the ass. "Just as long as you don't imagine that
you're kissing her husband," Jimi concluded with a laugh.

It started small but everyone laughed. Almost none for the
same reasons, but it was hearty bordering on hysterical.

Star laughed along, though she didn't really think it was

that funny; she was relieved and mystified that Jimi was taking it all so well. Perhaps wisely, she decided simply to leave
well enough alone.

While Operation Swedish Meatball was under way on the
work front, Star had been at work on a secret plan of her
own. To make a more solid commitment to their life together,
she'd decided to make getting the house ready priority one. It
was a great idea, except that, like it or not, Star already had at
least two other priorities—shooting two television shows a
week.

That meant, in the midst of the shoots, Star was having to
meet with decorators and contractors to approve samples,
colors, plans, and changes. Star found herself with more to do
than ever. But with the added demands of keeping up with the
house, she was even more overloaded. For the first time, she
resorted to some of the pills a bud of Jimi's had recommended
in the final days of *Hy Voltz* to pep her up once in a while. Not
every day, but when her schedule got too much.

Not only did she feel that she could get more done, she felt
more organized somehow. She could sit in the tub with a yel-
low legal pad and plan out a week's worth of work on the
house, then get on the phone, get it all delegated, then sleep it
off and get back to work. It was like magic. And magic can be
so tempting.

For the time being, it was working. Even their fear and
anxiety over Cabo subsided.

"Honey," Jimi called to her one rare evening when she'd returned home at a reasonable hour. "Come here and look at
this."

"What?" she called back from the kitchen, where she was making herself a smoothie. "What is it?" She walked into the den licking the honey off her finger, still carrying the jar. "You want a smoothie?"

"Look at this." He pointed at the screen.

"Oh, Jimi," Star said irritably. "You dragged me in here to look at porn? Whatever they're doing, I've seen it, or done it, or whatever." She turned to go.

"No, wait," Jimi said excitedly. "That's not it. Look at that guy there. With the nipple ring."

"The one who obviously dyes his hair?" Star asked, turning back, squinting her eyes and folding her arms.

"Oh, yeah, I guess you're right." He chuckled. "You notice anything else about him?"

"Aside from the obvious similarities to every man on earth?" Star said, hungry for her smoothie.

"Not just that," Jimi urged, taking her arm and leading her nearer to the huge screen she was having no difficulty seeing. "Look at his face."

"His face?" Star snorted, looking. "That's a novelty."

"Doesn't he look kind of like—"

"Oh my God!" Star said, sitting on the edge of the coffee table and covering her mouth. "It's the plumber."

"I knew it," Jimi howled, throwing himself onto the sofa beside her. "I thought it was."

"It's totally him."

The video and the smoothies were quickly forgotten, though not the honey. Star and Jimi loved honey. So much so that they had devised a game they called simply Honey. They took turns. Each would take the jar and put a spoonful of honey on his or her own body. The object was for the other to lick off the honey. They had discovered that you could lick and lick and lick and the honey would still be where you put it, so a couple of spoonfuls could go a really long way. Their plumber proved quite inspirational, and they used nearly half a jar.

Their porn star plumber was not the only interesting discovery that the renovation produced. Getting a permit for additions, Star was asked to sign some papers about the ownership of the house, about them and previous owners. She discovered that the house had once belonged to Vincent Ewer, the star of one of her all-time favorite movies, *Stolen Love*. It was the story of a man who while robbing a woman's home discovers her most private fantasies and then pretends to be the woman's ideal in order to win her love. But once he has that love, he begins to reveal his true self, and he is not at all the man she fell in love with.

But illusions were not the immediate trouble. Reality was causing Star far more problems.

Hy Voltz's holiday premiere was looming large. On the surface it was a joyous event, a big studio premiere of Star's first film. There was every reason to celebrate her big moment. Yet, in truth, the experience had left her with so many unpleasant memories it was hard to be excited, let alone celebratory.

On the plus side, a piece of music Jimi had written had been selected as the title theme, and it was something for him. More than anything else, she was happy about the opportunity to promote the sound track and Jimi's work. Jimi too seemed pleased about the event.

It was their first red carpet walk together. That is, it was the first time they had actually invited the paparazzi to take their picture together. The opening was held at the old, historic Chinese Theater on Hollywood Boulevard, the site of all those famous handprints and footprints in the cement out front. Star had not been to the Chinese since she'd first arrived in Hollywood and taken the irresistible trip over to see.

So returning to the spot for the opening of her first film was more than a little significant to her. Of course, she was wearing a lace-up rubber outfit, huge hair, and major eyeliner. Jimi had combed his unruly hair and slicked it back. In his tuxedo he looked more like a 1920s matinee idol than a wild man rock star, and it was all Star could do to let him out of the back of the limo as Lito drove them to the event.

"Later," she said, stealing one last kiss as they pulled up to the entry for the carpet walk.

"It's a date," he said, copping a squeaky feel.

The door flew open and the world rushed up to meet them.

The photographers were quickly sated with couple shots and soon began screaming out for Star alone.

Star was torn. It was work. She was there to draw as much attention to the event as possible. The best way for her to do that was to pose for the photos and do the interviews on the carpet. But fuck them, she decided, clutching Jimi's arm, she would take pictures only with Jimi, and too bad for a movie that had treated them both so shabbily.

When they got inside, she was held up by the producers, and Jimi went to get them something to drink. Jimi was well on the way to plastered by the time she caught up to him, though where he'd gotten enough to drink that fast she wasn't sure. The party wasn't until after. So, drunk in the car on the way home, he had canceled their date by passing out on the way inside and slept on the floor in the front hall.

The film fared much better than anyone expected, rocketing to number one.

The critics didn't agree, but to everyone's surprise—including Star and Jimi—the public couldn't get enough of *Hy Voltz,* which quickly became the highest-grossing film of the year. Even the sound track shot up the charts, with Jimi's theme song getting constant airplay.

It was as if Star couldn't make a mistake. But the increased scrutiny only served to heighten her fears that someone was going to find out what they'd done, which only drove the two of them more deeply into seclusion and—irony of ironies—only increased the paparazzi's appetite.

The only answer was escape of a different kind.

6

oh me, oh my

Jimi seemed happier. In the midst of the chaos of their home renovation he'd somehow managed to get the garage studio up and running. While there was nothing official yet, he'd been having a high old time jamming with his buds on tunes new and old. He even set up a little production company he called Jimiville after the name Star had given the house.

Star was pleased that Jimi was spending more time with his work, but between the two of them the party never stopped. There were always friends over and plenty of good times, but it was starting to take its toll on Star. Often, there were still people up from the night before when she left for work at 5 A.M.

Star was working two production jobs, and her hours did

not match those on the unwritten party invitations. So, in the credit column, Jimi was more occupied, leaving her on her own on the set. On the debit side, Star was catching up on her sleep in her trailer, her only refuge from the Hollywood Scene Stealers taking over her life.

The combination was wearing her down, but she wasn't sure how to fix it. If things got too quiet the paranoia and anxiety kicked in. Not to mention that she was actually having a great deal of fun when she didn't have an early call the next day.

Operation Swedish Meatball continued to work, as well, and even when Jimi was on the set, he was less jealous and suspicious of Star and her costar. Their on-screen romance was flourishing, and even the tabloid rumors of an offscreen romance between her and Sven only made Jimi laugh. Star was unaware of the hoax that was responsible for Jimi's change of attitude and just chalked it up to their party-like-a-rock-star lifestyle.

It was a tiring but good time. The only real sour note seemed only a little sharp at the time.

The party moved to Star's trailer as well. She regularly returned from the set to circumstances that to call unprofessional would be a massive understatement. Loud music, naked groupies, and more than one of the show's staff injured. One of the wardrobe ladies ended up getting divorced over a particularly spicy afternoon.

It meant that Billy, Skip, and Missy were almost constantly on set to look after Star's hair and makeup and to escape the goings-on in the trailer.

But it also strained Operation Swedish Meatball to the breaking point.

The romance between Star's and Sven's characters was really heating up. "When will BeeGee and Casey do it?" the tabloids and the fan magazines wanted to know. The romance had progressed well beyond the moonlight-kiss stage, but hadn't quite made it to the bedroom. Clearly, what had started as a little on-the-job flirtation between the two lifeguards was barreling toward the bedroom.

Jimi remained oblivious, even going so far as to try to fix Sven up with a record promoter who Jimi knew batted for Sven's team. Skip headed off the disaster and assured Jimi that Sven was seeing someone. Fortunately, that someone's name was Samantha, and Sven always called her Sam.

The double play saved the day temporarily, but ultimately doomed the game.

Jimi could ask about Sam and Sven could mention her without raising much suspicion, but only because Jimi and Sven didn't really talk much—until they discovered a shared fondness for that peculiarly L.A. obsession, the Lakers.

"We should have Sven and his partner over for game night sometime once the season starts," Jimi suggested to a distracted Star. "Or maybe we could all go to a game."

"Oh, I don't think so," Star said, only half-considering it as she checked herself in the trailer's makeup mirror following a quick bathroom break between takes. "Is Sven starting a business?"

"I don't know." Jimi shrugged. "Why do you ask?"

"You said his *partner.*"

"Oh, well, what's the right term?" Jimi turned his palms skyward. "*Lover, significant other?*"

"Aren't you formal?" Star eyed him in the mirror.

"Okay, Sam then." Jimi shrugged. "We never do anything with your friends. I thought it would be nice."

"That's sweet, honey, but really, we're not that close." She gave him a quick kiss as she headed out the door. "Anyway, I'd rather keep it that way. I feel like everyone here knows too much of my business as it is."

Sven was such a big Lakers fan and the series was doing so well that he treated himself to two courtside season tickets to the Lakers. At the price of a luxury sport coupe, the tickets were a celebrity indulgence.

For reasons defying logic outside the balance sheet, with no football team, the Lakers became L.A.'s official home team, attracting a veritable who's who of Hollywood royalty. The courtside seats are always filled with faces of those even more famous than the world champion team they come to watch. As a result, the cameras present are as likely to be focused on the stands as on the court.

And the cameras were at the ready when Sven took Sam to inaugurate his seats. Sven had already earned a spot on everyone's most-beautiful-people list, so when he showed up at the game with his girlfriend, the photos were an easy sale for the season-tipoff coverage. When Jimi spotted his beloved Lakers on the cover of *USA Today* and picked it up to get the highlights of the game, he also saw Sven's beloved Sam.

At first he looked at the guy on Sven's right, smiled, and thought what a nice-looking couple they made. But as he read and reread the caption, it became clear that *Sam* was short for *Samantha* and that Jimi had been played. He kept questioning it as he went over it in his mind. Had he simply been mistaken? Had he gotten the wrong impression?

Feeling hurt, deceived, and betrayed, Jimi blamed the only

two people who were only guilty of having amazing onscreen chemistry—Star and Sven. He also leaped to the conclusion that they must really have had something to hide to perpetrate such a massive deception. He jumped into the Ferrari and tore off to the set to have a word with his wife.

Lulled into a false sense of security, no one at *Lifeguards* reacted to the sound of squealing tires in the parking lot with anything other than mild annoyance. At worst they'd either have to retake the shot without the racket or loop it by having those in the scene rerecord their dialogue by lip-synching to get the noise out of the ruined take.

"Cut," Brock called irritably, preferring to retake the scene as he had notes anyway. "Okay, when the demolition derby is done up there, let's try it again. And this time, Sven, as you take her hand, I want you to be more tentative."

"Tentative," Sven repeated in a way that Brock knew meant Sven had no idea what the director was talking about.

"Look at her face like you've asked her a question," Brock went on, to avoid making his actor look foolish. "Will she come back to your apartment with you or not? That is unanswered here, and the viewers won't know what she's decided until the next scene with the two of you in the sack."

"I'll tell you what she's decided!" Jimi shouted from behind the camera crew, stalking forward awkwardly across the sand. "She's decided to come with me."

The crew immediately began acting busy to avoid seeming to watch the action that was unfolding between Star and Jimi.

"Jimi?" Star said. "What's wrong?"

"I just saw the pictures of Sam in *USA Today*," Jimi said, grasping Star's hand firmly to drag her away from the rest of the cast.

Sven was not only baffled and confused, but since Sam was his girlfriend, he felt oddly responsible.

"Sam's picture?" Star asked, clueless. "Have you been drinking?" she asked quietly.

"I'm sober," Jimi hissed.

"I'm missing something here," Star said quietly, still unsure what they were talking about. "I'm guilty of Sam's pictures? Baby, I'm worried about you."

"I'm not crazy!" Jimi shouted. "Although I was crazy to trust you in the first place, considering how we got together. How do you think it makes me feel to be deceived like this?"

"Is something wrong?" Sven asked absurdly, walking dangerously close to the ticking time bomb.

"I have no idea," Star confessed.

"Don't play innocent with me," Jimi bellowed, drawing back as if to take a swing at Sven as he came within striking distance. "Don't forget, I know the truth."

"Just what do you think I'm guilty of?" Star asked carefully.

"Like you don't know," Jimi growled disgustedly. "Do I have to spell it out for you?"

"Well, I'm not a very good speller." Star shrugged. "But I'll take whatever clues you've got."

"Sam is Sven's girlfriend," Jimi said as though he'd discovered the Holy Grail.

Star and Sven only stared at him expectantly, still waiting for it.

"That's it?" Star said finally when Jimi said no more.

"You owe me a hundred dollars," Billy said surreptitiously to Skip as Skip moved in to start the salvage operation.

"That's lunch," he called as he took Sven's elbow. "We need to do something with your hair."

A much relieved crew dispersed as they all but ran away from the setup.

"My hair?" Sven said, reaching information overload, what with Jimi's odd behavior and Brock's whole new "tentative" concept. He wondered why Jimi felt so strongly about Sam. Was he jealous? Was Jimi gay or bi or what was going on? Sven was in his trailer before he thought to ask any of these questions and soon became distracted with the touchups for the scene.

Star was not so lucky. Left standing on the beach to deal with Jimi's over-the-top reaction to something she knew nothing about, she tried once more to calm him and to figure out what he was talking about.

"Why are you so upset about Sven's girlfriend?" Star asked gently in the hopes of not setting him off again.

"You're fucking him, aren't you?" Jimi demanded.

"Why does the news that he has a girlfriend make you think I'm fucking him?" Star said, looking for a place to sit down.

"Are you?"

"Of course not." Star made her way toward the folding chairs just off camera.

"Then why all the lies?" Jimi said, grabbing her shoulder and spinning her back to face him.

"What lies?"

"Something's up. I'll figure it out." Jimi clenched his fists and made a noise that caused Star's blood to run cold. It reminded her of other men in her life. Star knew all too well this was the sound you hear before you get hit. Instinctively, she flinched, but instead of her, Jimi went after the folding chairs and coolers under the canopy in the break area.

"This innocent thing just makes it worse, Star," Jimi wailed, waving his finger in her face, tears of rage in his eyes. "Sven is not gay and you know it."

"Yeah, I do," Star said, sitting at last on one of the ruined coolers. "Did you think he was?"

"Don't act innocent," Jimi said, kicking at what was left of the craft services table. "The game is over, Star." He trampled potato chips and cookies under his boots. "Do you hear me? Over."

What had just happened? Star wondered as she picked up one of the Perriers out of the sand and opened it. Jimi's moods had always been unpredictable, but this one seemed to come completely out of nowhere. She worried that all the parties were catching up with them and that maybe something worse was going on. But most of all, she worried that the man she loved more than anything else in the world was way more upset with her than he'd ever been before. They had to trust each other.

They had to stay together.

She smiled as the answer came to her—a celebration of him. His birthday was coming up and it was the perfect excuse to throw him a party that would show him in ways that she knew he could understand just how much she loved him.

She wandered back toward the trailer as she began planning the extravaganza.

The show wrapped for the day, and when they resumed, there was a whole new script. Needless to say, the on-screen romance was derailed, however temporarily. Instead of their going back to Casey's place, they rewrote the script to have BeeGee spot a swimmer in distress and drop Casey's hand to run to the rescue. The answer to the tentative question turned out to be no, and the whole thing was posed as a tease. BeeGee thinks they should call it quits because the distraction at work endangers the lives of those they protect and serve. Casey still thinks they should get together or they'll be too distracted to do their jobs in the first place.

It was pure Velveeta, but the audience loved it and the show scored another ratings bonanza. But then, their audience really did love Velveeta.

At least that went smoothly.

"Fuck no. I just saw *Extra* zooming in on your kiss with Sven and I'm not coming with you," Jimi said, snatching his hand from hers as she pleaded with him, sobbing.

"But, Jimi, you have to," Star wailed, her voice echoing in their tennis-court-sized master bath.

She sat on the edge of the marble tub that might easily seat five, but was built just for two. It was where she had done most of the planning for the night that Jimi was threatening to ruin, because it was one of the few places where he would leave her alone. She was determined it was truly going to be a surprise party.

Following Jimi's strange overreaction on the set, he had been constantly at her side, watching her as if she were trying to escape. She did everything to try to reassure him, but it was to no avail. He saw malice in her every action and read deceit into her every word.

A suggestion that they go to a party or an event together

was met with questions of "Why?" and "Who's going to be there?" He could never seem to believe that it was only him that she wanted. So they'd stay home and he'd accuse her of being ashamed to be seen out with him.

She'd pinned her hopes on a surprise birthday party and hoped for the best.

It was the most elaborate thing she'd ever done or imagined doing in her life. She'd always loved the circus and had actually trained with Cirque du Soleil, so she was able to convince them to perform at the party. What she didn't know was that Jimi had checked up on her and found out she was lying when she'd told him she was going to the set or to a costume fitting to keep the party preparations secret.

Over one hundred performers were to entertain at a party with only twenty-five guests. She had hired a huge ranch on which to set up three massive circus-sized tents and had a full-scale light-up entry sign built to proclaim the fantasyland she had constructed in his honor—Jimiville. Beyond, a Ferris wheel and a merry-go-round played their haunting and seductive carnival music, and their lights brightened the wilderness that surrounded them. But the beacon would go unheeded unless she could change Jimi's mind.

The party was to be a private funfair, planted in the desert soil just for Jimi's pleasure. But because he'd become jealous and suspicious of all the sneaking around Star had had to do to put it all together, he was refusing to do the only thing he had to do to make the night a success.

Star had told him there was going to be a costume party for his birthday, but that was all she'd told him. She needed him to put on his crown and get in the car. That was it.

All her planning, time, and effort—not to mention the

hundreds of thousands of dollars—were about to go to waste. She felt helpless. She felt despair. And then she felt the fury of hell blaze bright in her chest. Her tears vanished, and she opened the bathroom door with a bang.

"Jimi," she shouted with enough threat to let him know he'd better answer.

"What?" he yelled back from what he called their rumpus room. He was lying on a massive two-man chaise that Star had chosen because it reminded her of the big chaise on the *Tits*. The use they had made of the new chaise had earned the little sitting room its raucous nickname.

"As I see it, you have two choices," Star said, standing firmly in the doorway, hands on hips.

"Oh, do I?" Jimi said.

"You can either get up, get dressed, and come with me to see for yourself why this is so important to me. You can divorce me tomorrow if it's not a good enough reason," Star said, waving one finger and then raising a second without waiting for a reply. "Or, you can sit right there and play video games. I don't know what to say to you anymore."

Twenty-eight minutes later, Lito held the door for Jimi as he belligerently climbed into the back of the car in full costume.

"Star, I'm warning you—"

"Not one word," she said with such force that Jimi actually stopped talking. "You can yell at me all the way home and I won't argue a bit. But on the way, not one word."

He was so angry that he actually remained silent, arms folded, teeth grinding.

Slowly his mood began to change.

First, at the restaurant he thought they were going to, he

met a group of twenty or so of his closest friends, all done up like characters from a Fellini film. They were already loaded onto a tour bus, filled with enough food and drink served by costumed midgets to be a party all on its own.

But his mood shifted from puzzled and bemused to awestruck as the bus rounded the corner on the dark mountain road and the huge JIMIVILLE sign illuminated the night and the glow of the funfair beyond came into view.

As they stepped off the bus, led by Jimi and Star, little people dressed as pawns unfurled a red carpet across the grass to meet their feet. The guests were greeted by naked dancers who tumbled across the lawn in a strange contortionist's dance.

An ice cream man pedaled his cart across their path ringing his bell.

"Welcome to Jimiville," Star announced, declaring the party officially begun.

It was a night of wild abandon and simple pleasures, like free rides on the Bavarian swings that spun the guests high into the air, and more sophisticated treats such as the laser projectors that beamed erotic shadows of groups having sex inside the tents. Topless models wearing painted-on clothes strolled among the guests with drinks and hors d'oeuvres.

Of course the music was amazing, and many of the famous musicians who were guests at the party joined in.

The action stopped throughout Jimiville at one point when a huge cannon drawn by naked men painted gold was brought to the center of the festivities. A hush fell over the crowd as a performer made up to be a very old man walked slowly through the gathering, dragging a huge ladder with the help of a band of the small people who were working the party. He leaned the ladder against the opening of the cannon and loaded himself into it. Then the little people drew away the ladder and lit the fuse with a torch.

With a wave of greeting to the crowd, the human cannon-ball slipped into the barrel. Moments later he was out again, fired over the heads of the crowd, over the tent and out of sight.

The music resumed and soon the revelers were back up to full speed.

The party reached a fever pitch with a frenetic dance number in which naked women were spun on a huge latex canvas while being slathered with paint by the hands of the guests and the other dancers who decorated them, smearing paint and glitter over naked flesh as the girls were spun faster and faster in time to the music.

The finale, a tribute to their wedding, came in the form of a company of Fat Elvis Impersonators singing "Volare" as they waved huge dildos at the wasted, painted, glittered crowd.

The Mighty Mouse cake was worn by the server.

And in an impassioned speech in which he said how much he loved his wife, Jimi pledged his undying love and devotion before, too drunk and heaven knew what else to stand any longer, he fell off the stage.

Full and under the influence, the crowd settled in to listen to the music. Jimi snuggled up next to Star, warm, content, and fortunately uninjured from his fall, all the jealousy and acrimony forgotten for that moment, and for good, Star hoped. When no one could eat one more bite or drink one more drink, the night was split by the peal of the bell on the ice cream cart as it twinkled by for the third and final time.

Star smiled, the perfect party was complete.

As if on cue, sirens intruded on the peaceful moment. A few guests were alarmed until they realized that a whole fleet of ambulances were lining up at the gate to take everyone home. A sign on the Jimiville bid farewell wih the message YOU'RE BEING VIDEOTAPED to the painted and glittered crowd.

"I love you, Jimi," Star said, taking his hand. "You know that? Just you."

"I love you too," Jimi said.

She wasn't sure her plan had worked or that he'd even remember it all. But it was one hell of a party.

7

can't you see?

"Look, Star," Stan said, catching up to her in the parking lot as she was leaving the set one day. "We can't keep this up."

"Well, there's always Viagra." Star giggled.

"I'm serious," Stan said, trying to be stern and failing miserably.

"I am too," Star said with a firm nod that made him smile.

He put a paternal arm around her shoulder as he walked her to her car. "It's like this. I need to get this shot and you need to deal with Jimi. I know that it makes Jimi crazy, but we have to get these two characters together."

"I'll see what I can come up with," she said as she vaulted up behind the wheel of her SUV. "Maybe we can take him out in the woods and leave him there. By the time he finds the gingerbread house or the three bears' porridge, we'll have the show in the can for the year."

"Thanks, Star." Stan waved as she backed out.

She smiled and waved as the window closed between them. She had no idea what to do. And she didn't have time to think about it. She had to get across town for *Hammer Time,* then meet her brother, Hank, who was coming out for his first visit now that the big Malibu house was finished and she had a place for him to stay.

Hank's trip was perfectly timed. Star had been invited to a party at the home of R&B music star Jean Soames. It was the sort of thing Jimi wouldn't be caught dead at, but Hank, who was no R&B fan, couldn't have cared less, as it was a Hollywood Party.

After *Hammer Time,* Star had just enough time to pick up Hank at "Lax," as she still called it.

"Who are you now, the tour guide?" Hank laughed as she pointed out the blimp field on the way up PCH as they headed toward home.

"No, I'm just your big sister and I'm older and smarter than you, dumb ass. Don't act lame at this party tonight, now."

"Don't worry about me," Hank snorted. "I've been living in the thriving metropolis of Florida City, I'll have you know."

The Soames house did not disappoint. Star's first stop in L.A. had been the French-château-styled Mann Castle, which was tough to top. But the Jean Soames place was pretty impressive, and Star was certain that it more than topped anything on Hank's regular party list.

It was one of those loosely referred to "architectural" L.A. houses. A cross between adobe mission and ultramodern, the place was all blinding-white stucco, blue glass, and water. Flat-roofed and stacked like building blocks, the house was behind a high wall sitting on a ledge on the hill overlooking West Hollywood, where Star had lived when she'd come to town.

"Look," she said, pointing from the hillside view as they walked down the drive to the front door. "There's the Bel Age. That's the hotel where I stayed when I first came to town."

"Hello," an extremely attractive young man, wearing little more than a smile, greeted them at the front door. "Everyone's out by the pool."

"Thanks," Star said flirtatiously. "Where are you headed?"

"I'm just here to answer the door." He smiled graciously. "Let me know if there's anything else you need."

"Okay," she said, heading across the large, mostly glass living room. Skylights made the all-white room glow in the late-afternoon sun. The glass curtain wall that comprised one entire side of the room opened onto a startling blue-tile infinity pool that floated like a sapphire in the blaze of sunset.

"Star," Jean called, spotting her and throwing his arms open wide in greeting. He made his way across the blue-tiled patio pursued by two young men wearing shorts with suspenders over their shaved and polished chests. "And who is this little confection you've brought?"

"Jean, this is my little brother, Hank. "Hank, this is Jean Soames."

"How do you do, sir," Hank said, taking Jean's hand. "It's an honor."

"My pleasure." Jean took Hank's hand in both of his. "I've always been very partial to little brothers. And these are O'Neil and Bartok, my little brothers, tonight anyway. This is—"

"Oh, Star Wood Leigh," one of the two gushed, taking Star's hand. "I'm a huge fan."

"I'm an air conditioner," Star replied, laughing at her own joke.

"I'm a big fan too," said the other one, giggling along with her.

"Now, boys," Jean said, giving both their tightly clad backsides a smack. "No starfucking. Well, not yet, anyway."

"I'm sorry, just so very pleased to meet you," one said.

"Likewise," his bookend concurred.

"Why don't you get them some drinks while I get Star and her little brother situated in the gazebo?"

"He doesn't look that little to me," the talkative one said, earning another smack.

Drink orders were taken. Jean, Hank, and Star made their way slowly to the gazebo on the far side of the pool overlooking West Hollywood below, and much of Los Angeles and even Long Beach beyond. They were delayed as they stopped to greet a who's who of Hollywood from the music industry and otherwise.

"There certainly are a lot of good-looking guys here," Star said once they were situated and Jean had left them to find out what had become of their drinks.

Hank snorted with laughter.

A number of beautiful women were present, but they were getting surprisingly little attention.

Star and Hank laughed pretty much through the whole party.

Perhaps the best thing that happened at the party was that

Star met avant-garde photographer Eric Marmont and his protegée. She had admired his off-beat style and vision, and the two instantly connected. While Hank was busy winning an impromptu limbo contest, Star and Eric were busy planning their spread for *Blab,* the edgy magazine which Warhol once edited. Star would pose as the corpses in a series of famous murders. They called it "want to chalk about it."

Though neither artist nor model realized it at the time, it was the beginning of a life-long partnership.

Star loved having Hank out for a visit; she kept finding reasons for him to stay a little longer. So, when he confided he'd like to stay on, Star was more than happy to help him get started. He moved into her old place, as she'd not gotten around to selling it yet. Actually, she hadn't tried very hard, as she enjoyed having her own little getaway when Jimi or work or whatever got to be too much. There was room for Hank at the house, but he was getting under Jimi's nails a bit, plus Hank had limited their sexual exploration and conquest of the house and all its rooms and flat surfaces. More to the point, Star thought Hank would do better with a little independence. He promised to find work and get a place of his own as soon as possible, but there was no rush as far as Star was concerned.

It was nice to have Hank around to remind her who she was and where she came from. And what was really important.

There were so many things to be valued in Hollywood that it was hard to keep account. Was it the awards or the money or the fame or the attention or the looks or the career? The checklist on a Hollywood scorecard was endless enough to keep the richest and most beautiful people hungry and motivated. No matter how spectacular the life—and whole television networks were devoted to describing the spectacular lives of the city's most glittering inhabitants—someone always seemed to have it better. So, having Hank in her life was like having an anchor to keep her in port when she was buffeted by the winds of outrageous fortune.

Though she didn't know it and couldn't have predicted it, a squall was shaping up.

She had given careful consideration to the *Lifeguards* dilemma. She wanted to be honest with Jimi, but he wanted to hear only what he wanted to hear.

In the end, Hank's down-home sensibilities won the day.

He overheard a phone conversation Star had with Theresa and picked up enough to figure out what was going on.

"You want a beer?" he called to her after she'd hung up.

"Root beer," she called back.

"Here you go," he said, cracking one for her, his own long-neck tucked under his arm. "You know, it's none of my business . . ."

"I know it isn't," she said, afraid of what was coming.

"All's you really have to do is make arrangements for him to be somewhere else when you shoot the scenes. Just make sure that he's not there."

"Isn't that deceptive?"

"Maybe." Hank shrugged, taking a pull off his beer.

Perhaps the most original idea had come from her costar Sven. Though he was still as in the dark about the Swedish Meatball conspiracy as Star, he was much better informed about the whole situation since Jimi's big scene at the shoot.

"Why don't we just get it over with," he suggested, his sparkling blue eyes glinting at her from his top-ten-most-beautiful face.

Star laughed it off, but the irony of the situation was not lost on her. She was actually being persecuted for something she wasn't doing, even though she easily could have . . . and it would hardly have been unpleasant. It had crossed her mind, but Sven was just a little too clean-cut for her tastes.

Hank was working as an extra on *Hammer Time*. In fact, like many newcomers to Hollywood he got his union membership card doing walk-on parts. And like all but about 5 percent of the members of SAG, he barely made enough to cover gas to the shoots, let alone to support himself.

On this particular day he was hanging around Star's dressing room at the end of a long production day. Star was giving him a ride home, as he did not yet have a car, and they talked as she got ready to leave. She did not have the kind of personal crew on *Hammer Time* that she did on *Lifeguards,* so it was just the two of them as she got out of makeup and costume on her own.

"Have you heard from Mom?" she asked, still waiting to hear back from her mother. She had suspected that her father was just not passing the messages along, at first, anyway. But too many were unreturned.

"Nah," Hank said, leafing through a magazine and not really paying attention.

"When was the last time she called you?" Star put her costume on the rack for the wardrobe lady to pick up.

"Not exactly sure." Hank looked up from a spread on NASCAR drivers.

"Hank, be serious," Star said irritably as she sat at the makeup table to survey what, if any, of Billy's work she wanted to take off before heading home. She frequently got her makeup done by her personal crew on *Lifeguards* before coming to the *Hammer Time* set, where she was at the mercy of the general cast crew—they were good, they just weren't Skip, Billy, and Missy.

"I am serious," Hank said, going back to his magazine. "And I kind of prefer it that way. She's always bossing me about something."

"I just wanted her advice," Star explained.

It was an unreasonable but manageable level of stress.

And then the world just completely went out of control.

Star had called her mother once again, and was surprised when her grandmother Gitta answered the phone.

"When will they be back?" Star asked, confused as to why Mama Gitta was there if her parents weren't home.

"Oh, I don't rightly know," Brigitta said in a singsong kind of way she had when she was nervous.

"Where have they gone?" Star said, growing tired of the runaround and determined to track her mom down.

"Well, that's the thing," her grandma said evasively.

"What's the thing? What's going on there?" Star said, getting anxious. "Are they all right, is everything okay?"

"Well," the old woman said, drawing it out, clearly deciding how to answer, "Star, your mom's in the hospital. She's had another attack."

"*Another* attack?" Star shrieked, unaware of any attacks.

"She can't walk at all anymore." Brigitta sighed sadly. "And the doctors say that without the surgery she never will again, and even then . . ."

It was more than Star could take.

Her mother's illness gave Star something to focus on at a time when she needed it most.

The couple, already the darlings or the target, depending

on how you looked at it, of every tabloid and paparazzi, and they followed Star to Cedar Sinai Hospital in Beverly Hills, where Star had her mother transported to get her the best specialists and find out what could be done.

Much to Lucille's—Star's mother's—dismay, her arrival at the hospital made the evening news. "I've never been on TV or had my picture in the paper in my life," she said disgustedly as she was wheeled into the hospital. "And they wait until I've got two weeks' worth of bed head, I'm strapped to a gurney, and have tubes sticking out of my nose."

"Is this what you have to do to make it in Hollywood nowadays?" Lucille joked through her oxygen mask.

"I don't know," Star said, taking her hand. "I do know it's the first time I got you out here for a visit."

The two women laughed until they cried.

Lucille never said, but she was plenty scared. And Star was overwrought and terrified over the developments surrounding her mom's health.

She turned her full attention to her mother's condition. It was serious and life-threatening. Her mom had lost the ability to walk because her circulatory system was so devastated by her years of chain-smoking. She simply didn't have the strength.

Star had always kidded that she was a committed secondhand smoker. She had never even tried smoking herself, but her mom and many of Star's boyfriends over the years were big-time smokers.

Her mom's problem had a surgical solution, but it was invasive and risky. However, the alternative was for her mom to spend the remainder of her brief life strapped to an oxygen tank, never to walk again.

There was also the cost, and Lucille had no insurance. For the first time, Star was truly grateful for her success. She simply wrote the hospital a check for the hundreds of thousands needed for the procedure.

And so, the surgery was scheduled, but it was far from a sure thing.

Star wanted to commit her time and resources full-time to taking care of her mom.

"This is another fine mess you've gotten me into, young lady," Lucille called to her daughter as she was wheeled off to surgery, delirious from all the medications they'd given her for the procedure.

"I'll be right here waiting for you," Star said, trying to act brave, but not doing a very good job of it as she walked alongside the gurney wheeling through the halls of the hospital. "You get better, you hear? I can't do this without you."

Lucille reached out and took her daughter's hand.

"You can do anything you want," Lucille said, giving a little squeeze. "Remember, it's your choice who you are. I'll be watching, whatever happens. I love you, Star."

Their hands separated as they reached the operating room doors and Star was left behind.

"You just get well, old woman," Star said, releasing her mother's hand and blowing a kiss after her. "I love you, Mom," she called, waving as Lucille passed through the swinging double doors into the land of authorized personnel only. The tears came as soon as her mom was out of sight. Once she felt she didn't need to be strong for her mother, Star collapsed onto the cold tile outside the OR doors.

8

no excuses

Lucille's funeral was a small family affair in the mainland cemetery just north of her home on Arcady Key. The bereaved were outnumbered four to one by members of the media.

Star was too devastated to notice the hyenas. All she could think of were her mother's final words.

"Remember, it's your choice who you are. I'll be watching, whatever happens."

The events of the past few months just kept playing over and over in her head. If only she could take them back. If only she could undo it all.

As they made their way to the cars after the graveside service, a photographer who must have slipped past security and hidden in a tree in the cemetery, dropped out of the branches into their path, shouting at them to "look this way," "give us a wave good-bye to mama." Blind with rage, Rick went after the man, catching him by the ankles as he tried to make his getaway over the fence, and dragged him facedown across the lawn and down the drive to the main gates.

"Dad, stop, you really need to stop!" Star shouted, trying to bring her father to his senses, but understanding his rage.

"The hell with that," Richard said, holding the flailing man up by his ankles. "Jimi, come open this goddamned gate and I'll give them a good-bye picture."

"I'm with you, Rick," Jimi said, dragging open the cemetery gates that had been kept closed to prevent just such intrusions.

As the broad metal panels rolled to one side, the press surged forward, stepping back as (to the edification of those present, not to mention newspaper buyers around the world) Star's father pitched the man down the drive, smashed his camera and tossed what remained of it after him.

"Leave my family alone," he said, waving an appropriately Neanderthal fist as the gates closed like a great steel curtain on his world debut performance.

Jimi gave him a high five of approval, which the press captured as the gates ground shut. Star was both upset and pleased. She was horrified that her mother's funeral had come to this, but how else could they react?

Sorry, Mom, but fuck them, she thought. To hell with the consequences.

"Tell me what's the difference between that man in the tree and anyone else in the world breaking in here?" her father asked, genuinely.

"He had a camera around his neck," Star shrugged.

"So that's the only difference between a stalker and a re-porter?" her father asked incredulously.

"Apparently," Star said, patting her father on the shoulder.

"Well, that's crazy." Rick wagged his finger. "I'll tell you, Star, you say the word, I make one phone call, and they just start disappearing."

Star and Jimi shared a knowing look behind her father's back.

"Jimi," Star said as they dragged the heavy-duty garbage bag through darkness.

"I couldn't agree with you more," Jimi said as they emerged in the darkness from the bushes onto the fairway of the unfinished golf course. "But they just won't leave us alone."

"That's not what I meant," Star sighed.

"Come on," he urged her. "Our flight leaves in an hour."

Star wondered if her mom was watching.

"Okay, on three," Jimi said, picking up one end and di-recting Star to get the other. "One, two, three."

The heavy bag splashed into the water, bubbling at the sur-face for a moment before it sank. There was another splash and then a couple more from the other side of the murky water hazard.

"What's that?" Star hissed, again horrified that they would be found out.

"The gators will be eating good tonight," Jimi chuckled as he took Star's hand and they made their way back to their rental car.

Things were just not the same when they got back to L.A.

The work was the same, the shows were the same, the twenty-four-hour party was the same, but something inside had shifted. It was as if she had been nearsighted and suddenly put on a new pair of glasses. The harsh new clarity made the world ugly and unbearable.

She would sit with Mutley in her room, in his favorite chair. He could stare out to sea for hours at a point beyond the horizon that only he seemed to see.

"What is it, boy?" Star said, snuggling up to him. "What's out there?"

Mostly, she just missed her mom, their conversations, her slightly cracked advice that always turned out exactly right. But life, flavorless as it had become, did not allow her much time for mourning.

Their personal life was not what it had been, either. Star was tired and exhausted most of the time, and Jimi was more and more frequently drunk to the point of passing out. If they went out, they were hounded by the press, which made him furious, which meant that he'd get so drunk that it didn't matter anymore. Some nights, he'd just pass out in the car and Star would leave him there to sleep it off. On his not-so-good nights, he'd bring his plans for revenge, belligerence, and anger into the house. The stress of it all was hurting their relationship.

Still, the sex, when it happened, was as fiery as ever, and Star preferred getting him to stay home rather than go out to play. She became quite the provocateur, surprising him wearing only a string of pearls or Gucci lingerie, or showing up in the bedroom with a whip.

One area that they had tried before and which they unsuccessfully tried again brought Star to seek expert advice.

"Missy," Star said one day when the Fab Four, as the little team called themselves, were alone in the trailer. "Would you go find Sven and tell him that I'd like to run the scene with him, if he has a chance?"

"Okay, sure," Missy agreed suspiciously, since no one on *Lifeguards* ever ran scenes. She was technically Billy's assistant and responsible for on-set makeup continuity, and Star was respectful of that, though occasionally she'd ask her for a favor. Missy gave Billy a questioning look.

"It's okay," Billy said, shooting Missy a you-got-me look behind Star's back. "I'll be fine. It's an easy morning."

"Thanks, Missy," Star said, "I really appreciate it."

Missy figured she'd get the dirt from Billy later, so she went with a knowing smile.

"No problem, Star," she called, leaving the trailer.

"Okay, what was that about?" Skip asked, taking the pins from his mouth.

"Well, I need to get you guys' *advice* about something," Star said tentatively, not sure of how to bring it up.

"Our advice?" Billy questioned, more suspicious still. "We do your hair and makeup."

"How do you fuck up the ass?" she blurted, unable to think of a more politically correct way to ask. "Give me details."

"What?" Billy laughed.

"Well," Skip snorted. "I guess you have come up with one other area where we might have a little insight."

"A little?" Billy was getting progressively more amused. "I gotta know, what is it that you want to know? *Do we?*"

"Well, really, *how* do you?" Star asked sheepishly. "I kinda figured from some of your jokes that . . . that you do. Jimi wants to, so I figured I'd come to the experts."

"Then you'll want to talk to Billy," Skip said archly.

"Hey!" Billy exclaimed.

"Well, I just figure you're going to have the experience she'll need in this arrangement," Skip said, raising his shoulders practically to his ears. "I could maybe advise Jimi."

"So, you're the boy?" Star asked Skip, delighted to talk about someone's sex life other than her own.

"We're both boys," Billy snorted.

"Well, he's the boy and I'm the man," Skip said, earning a crack with a wet towel.

"Okay," Star said, rolling her eyes. "If everyone in the entire world gets to talk about my sex life, you two can talk about yours in the privacy of the trailer without turning into a couple of thirteen-year-olds."

"All right," Billy said, sobering up. "It's called bottom and top." He pointed at himself and then Skip.

"Or passive and active," Skip said, pointing at Billy and then himself.

"Too clinical," Billy said, wrinkling his nose. "Pitcher and catcher."

"I like that one," Star said. "It sounds fun, like a game."

"Well, then, Miss Star," Skip said, taking her hand, "meet Billy, the biggest catcher in the league."

Billy threw the wet towel over Skip's head.

Star's phone rang with the opening strains of "Can't You See," and she checked the number. "It's the lawyer. Excuse me a minute."

Star listened, then rolled her eyes as he explained the latest lawsuit, this one from a producer who claimed she backed out of a film she'd merely read the script for. "Tell him to take a number," she sighed, before turning back to Billy.

"All right, what do you want to know?" he asked, taking the makeup chair beside hers.

"Well, like everything," Star said, throwing up her hands.

"It requires preparation and practice," Billy said. "Straight boys and tops live in the delusion of spontaneity."

"Oh, please," Skip said, waving the conversation away.

"He just wanted to stick it in, right?" Billy said, not looking at Skip at all.

"Pretty much." Star nodded, then sipped her coffee.

"Typical," Billy sniped, folding his arms. "Well, first off, some bad news. Being a girl, you're never going to enjoy butt sex quite as much as boys do. It's a design thing."

"Boys are designed for butt sex?" Star said, her eyes widening.

"Surprising, huh?" Billy said with a little grin.

"You know, you hear it's unnatural."

"Not a bit. You remember the little hint I gave you about the come-hither finger up the chute during blow jobs?" Billy asked seriously. "Well, that's Mr. Prostate you're tickling. Only boys have them, and they get really tickled during butt sex. Not every guy wants to, but it's the same for all boys."

"Me, for instance," Skip said, raising his hand.

"Yeah, we all got that, butch," Billy said with an exasperated sigh. "But for boys who do, there's plenty of good reason built right in."

"It's all part of God's plan," Skip said derisively.

"Don't mock." Billy raised a warning finger. "I could have a really bad headache for a few months."

"It's a beautiful thing, Star," Skip said sincerely.

"But not for girls?" Star questioned.

"I didn't say that." Billy patted her hand. "Plenty of girls like it too, as I understand it. It's just a question of technique and personal preference. Straight boys and tops alike can learn a little thing called the reach-around."

"A hand job?" Star asked.

"During," Billy said, giving Skip a meaningful look. "It can go a long way toward improving the experience for both parties by motivating the catcher."

"Got it," Star said. "Jimi never minds that."

"Lucky girl," Billy said, rolling his eyes. "Now, the rest is all about preparation."

"Stretching exercises?" Star asked. "My mom was big on Kegel exercises, where you spread your legs and sit on the floor and try to suck up the carpet."

"You should show Billy how to do those," Skip teased.

"Douche," Billy said, pointedly ignoring him.

"Back there?"

"Yeah, you can get little enema bottles all ready to go at the drugstore. They're pretty self-explanatory and they're reusable with plain warm water. Just a tip, though. You do not have to lie on the floor and pull your leg up to your chest like it shows on the diagram."

"Though that's an excellent position for getting started later," Skip mused.

"Well, yeah, that's actually true," Billy agreed after first looking for and not finding an argument. "But the best way to begin, as with all things sexual, is with a little foreplay. If you're all nice and clean, and some people shave too, it's a matter of taste."

"Well, you all remember how they had to glue it on to give me pussy hair," Star said, breaking up at the memory.

"Oh, that's right," Skip said, cackling. "I remember that. It was so hideous. Marsten is so weird about that."

"And that poor little guy," Billy said, recalling the beard maker. "I felt bad for him, but he was such a professional."

"Anyway," Star said, riding over the digression, "shaving won't be a big issue for me."

"Right," Billy said. "And Jimi, he's good about oral sex in general?"

"I married him, didn't I?" Star said with laughter.

"Well, the same technique applies here, and, girl," Billy said, taking her hand, "it'll make you scream."

Skip nodded his head and put his fingers in his ears.

"Then he works in a lubed-up finger, and then two to get the lube in and the idea started. This is the part where having a prostate comes in handy, so you'll have to find your own ways to improvise," Billy said, not entirely sure of the mechanics involved. "And then the big show. Now, you can actually practice beforehand with your own fingers or with a dildo."

"Practice?" Skip snorted. "Is that what we're calling it now?"

"Or a vibrator if you've got one," Billy went on, pretending not to hear.

"If?" Star laughed. "One?"

"Okay, well, just get him to go slow at first," Billy forged ahead. "Easy in and then wait. You can breathe or even push like you would if you were, you know, using those muscles down there ordinarily, but the main thing is just to relax. It's not going to injure you; the pain is just because you're not used to it. Once you relax and get going, it all changes. And with a good reach-around or, better still, if you're facing just a plain old hand job, you'll forget that it ever bothered you in the first place."

"Aw, what a touching mother/daughter moment," Skip said, batting his eyes foolishly.

"You make fun," Billy said, "but I can't remember a single complaint."

"If I can add something," Skip said, putting an arm around Billy in a sideways hug, "Jimi'll love it if you kind of squeeze your cheeks together."

"Like you're trying to hold a fart." Billy nodded with an embarrassed shrug.

"Oh my God!" Star shrieked with laughter.

"When he's pulling, not pushing," Skip added, reaching over and holding up Billy's hand by a diamond-and-sapphire ring. "Trust me on this one, he'll really, really love it."

"Is that how I got that ring?" Billy asked, startled and unsure exactly how to react.

"It sure didn't hurt," Skip said with a knowing smile.

Star got a diamond necklace a week later.

Maybe it was just a coincidence.

9

nobody's fault

Going out to celebrate had seemed like a good idea at the time.

The nightclub Ka Mano, in fact, partly belonged to Star, so she would have some measure of control over the situation. She had been out of the house only to go to work and to court, and Jimi didn't have a gig, so he had been pacing the confines of Jimiville like a caged cat. They had indulged in their singular recreation until they had worn each other raw. Even with Skip and Billy's tip and their own wild imagination there was only so much they could do.

So they arranged an Ecstasy party to shake off the mood with sweat, love, and rock and roll.

She wore a rubber dress, so naturally the party declared

her the dominatrix. She had everyone skip into the bar past the phalanx of photographers banked there in anticipation of the moment. Even Jimi didn't get upset, as they were already rolling on X and too busy being ridiculous to care what the press did or said. Once inside, she decreed that it was topless night, but with a twist. The men would go topless and entertain the women. The decree soon became unenforceable, but not before most every man in the place had shed his shirt.

Along with the X, which made the most of all the exposed flesh, their neighbor Enoch had brought enough speed to keep the celebration in high gear, virtually indefinitely. With a bottomless bar tab and Star the owner there to keep the place open as long as they cared to play, it became quite a night.

Mack Wraith, a musician friend, was the first to start dancing on the tables, which he did most ably, including a glassware-shattering finale that cleared the table. Star did backflips, wiping out once or twice on the wet tables in heels.

Jimi hit Star's black rubber bodice with a cigarette and it exploded, rolling up her body like a window shade. Women throughout the club, long since closed to the public, followed her lead.

As the party made its way back out to the car in the early-morning hours, a photographer ran into Star's breast, his lights blinding her. She looked back as Jimi grabbed the stooped man by his camera, yanking him forward with the strap still securely around the photographer's neck. As the photog struggled, Jimi began spinning him around like some wild dervish, trying to wrench the camera free. Eventually it slipped over the photographer's head, and Jimi raised it into the air and smashed it to the pavement like Moses and the tablets. The photographer took a dive and rolled down a steep hill. It might have ended there, but one of the photographers pulled a canister of pepper spray from his pocket and sprayed Jimi and Star in the face.

It was like gasoline on a fire.

As Mack, Enoch, and Lito tried to help a wailing Star into the back of the Escalade, Jimi charged, taking their attacker down and pounding his head onto the carpeted pavement. Jimi was completely out of control, and as the photographer's colleagues merely watched and got the sexy shots, Jimi took out weeks of rage. Here was an enemy he could find and face. One neck he could twist. One battle he could win. Mack and Enoch dragged him off the bloody man and had to wrestle and fight with Jimi to get him into the car.

Star too was out of control, screaming over and over again for everyone to "fuck off." The press went wild, and the entire event was caught on tape, launching a weekly television series on the cable entertainment channel featuring unflattering candid moments of famous people provoked by the paparazzi.

After their escape from the nightclub riot, Star's and Jimi's eyes still burning from the spray, they pulled over into a residential yard and borrowed the sleeping owner's hose to wash it off.

The incident further served to unite the two against the world outside. "Everyone sucks but us" became their motto.

Perhaps the only ray of sunshine was a benefit concert in New York that Star's favorite cause, the Brotherhood for Animals Gaining Legal Equality—B.A.G.L.E.—was hosting. Jimi's band was to play along with a host of ultrafamous rock icons. Star could not have been happier about it.

Billy and Skip were not fooled.

"So," Billy teased, "your pet charity is having a concert on the other side of the country?"

"And it just happens to be on the very same night that you're shooting the big love scene with Casey?" Skip said, clicking his tongue. "Star and Sven are sitting in a tree . . ."

"K-I-S-S-I-N-G," the two chanted together. "First comes love, then comes divorce, then comes Jimi with his day in court."

"Funny," Star said, not amused by the joke nor admitting any complicity in the scheduling of the concert.

"I'm sorry, honey," Billy said, patting the back of her hand indulgently. "Not feeling well?"

"How's your head?" Skip asked, an exaggerated expression of concern on his face as he leaned down next to her, their cheeks almost touching.

"Well, I haven't had any complaints yet," Star said, cracking up.

In honor of the momentous reunion of Fools Brigade for the big concert, there was to be a big do out at Jimiville. It was Jimi's deal and Star decided she would let him plan it.

She would only be a guest at this party.

She had a shoot the day of the festivities and had planned to drop in with some friends from work and join the evening in progress. The shoot ran late and her work friends bowed out, so by the time she returned home the party was well under way. Fueled by the usual better living through chemistry, the party made out-of-hand seem like a Sunday-school social.

The front hallway was filled with people in varying states of undress, seated on the steps and hanging over the banister above. Those who weren't making out were watching a couple of kids with guitars doing their own variations on whatever was blaring on the house sound system. As Star made her way past the miniconcert, which was no small task, she found the living room filled with a pack of Hollywood Scene Stealers and every manner of vice. You name it and you had only to look behind a few pieces of furniture to find it, from all-but-full-on sex to every recreational application of most every substance known to man. The speed freaks were grinding their jaws, dancing, playing some kind of game, and talking all at the same time. The potheads were either smoking or eating or giggling or some combination of the three. The heroin chics were nodding out. And the cokeheads were talking as fast at they could, mostly to the nod-outs and potheads, who were not really listening but not interrupting. The drunks were mostly fighting among themselves.

Not spotting Jimi right away, Star climbed the kitchen stairs up to her room, which, along with every other bedroom and bathroom, was in use by couples horny from all the mood generators downstairs. She threw everyone out of her bedroom and locked the door against further intruders. She wanted to be mad, but she'd known whom she was married to when she told him he was in charge of the party.

Tired, Star opened the door to her bathroom. All she wanted was to clean up a bit from a strenuous day at the beach and try to catch a second wind so she could join the mayhem already in progress downstairs. She paused as she heard the all-too-familiar noise of what sounded like at least two couples doing she knew exactly what. One of them was her brother, Hank, who was snorting coke off the ass of one of the girls.

"Unh-huh," Star cleared her throat without looking too closely. "Excuse me."

There was a small scream, some scrambling, and then JC,

Hank, and Theresa emerged with two other young women wearing Star's best bath towels.

"Hi, Sis." Hank grinned, his face flushed and his pupils dilated.

"Hi, Hank, Theresa," Star grinned back. Her little brother was growing up. "You kids need to find a new playroom."

"Yeah, sure," JC agreed, hustling everyone toward the door. "See you downstairs, Star." Theresa grinned.

"There's a sauna off the changing rooms by the pool," Star said, amazed that it was her house she was talking about.

"Sure thing, thanks," JC called over his shoulder, pulling the door closed behind them.

It reopened as another small group poked their heads in, looking for a space.

"Occupied," Star said, crossing to relock the door.

"May we join you?" an attractive young surfer with shaggy blond hair asked, his treacherously beautiful blue eyes locking with hers.

"Private party," she said, pushing the door closed and turning the latch. But if she hadn't been a married lady, she'd surely have yanked blue eyes inside before she'd locked the door. She had to laugh at herself as she looked out the back window and saw the orgy that was evolving in the pool and hot tub. She'd have to point blue eyes out to Jimi later.

She was still laughing to herself as she headed for the privacy of her bathroom. She smiled as she remembered how Roberto, whom she'd worked with on the Cabo shoot, had become so sexually obsessed with Jimi that he'd broken into the house one night when he knew Star was working late and Jimi was alone. Creeping into that very room, he had awakened Jimi with promises of the best blow job he'd ever had.

As always, Jimi woke up horny and ready to go, so with a shrug he agreed and the deal was struck. The comforter was tossed aside and Roberto moved in to close the deal when Jimi spotted the braces on Roberto's teeth.

"Whoa, tiger," Jimi said, pulling the comforter back up to cover his hard-on.

"What's wrong?" Roberto asked, still panting with excitement.

"Dude, head's head but those braces might tear my shit up," Jimi said giving his intruder a friendly pat on the shoulder before turning over and going back to sleep.

She had to laugh and she had to love him. It wasn't that he was a married man, it wasn't the blow job from another guy, and it wasn't even the breaking and entering that put her man off. It was the braces. She laughed and thought again about blue eyes and wondered what Jimmy would say; after all, it was a party.

After the shower she put the dogs away out of concern for what they might pick up off the floor, and went in search of Jimi.

When she finally found him, he was in the studio at the keyboard with Fools Brigade doing what he loved best. Star would have liked to think it was second best, but she doubted it and that was okay. She sat and listened and watched for a while. He looked so happy and complete.

Darien and Joshua, bass and guitar, had been in high school with Jimi. Fools Brigade had started in Jimi's parents' garage, and they were still playing, as they had back when Jimi's father had enclosed and soundproofed the carport in self-defense. Vic, the drummer, had joined them a bit later, after they'd quit school to follow their dream to the Sunset Strip music scene and follow in the footsteps of their idols.

They were grown men now and had reached an age when most men in their field were either dead from the excesses of the life or slipping into obscurity. Some few, if they were smart, lived on the investments made during their salad days. Some, like the Stones, stayed on to become legends. And some just refused to leave the stage, even though the audience had long departed. You never knew which it was until you were being voted into the hall of fame or a made into a punch line.

Which it turned out to be hardly mattered at that moment.

Star knew how happy Jimi looked pounding out their old hits, his drink untouched and melting, his hands busy. What she didn't know was that playing together was all that was still possible for the group. Whether or not they'd been on-stage too long, they had been together too long, and the minute they stopped playing, they started fighting. But Star couldn't tell by looking. She only saw Jimi's joy as his fingers found the familiar keys. Eventually she went and joined him on the bench, resting her head on his shoulder as he played on into the night.

When they finally took a break, he kissed her and before she could say anything at all and put her at ease. "I have no idea who all these people are," he said quietly into her ear. "I invited about twenty or thirty of the usual suspects, and this is who showed up. They had to have the gate code to get in, so it was an inside job. I'm thinking Hank and JC?"

"Or Theresa; I caught them upstairs in our bathroom." She grinned, nodding. "I didn't know they were that close."

"The candy man is everybody's best friend," Jimi said knowingly. "I think they knew each other from back home. Or maybe they just had that in common."

"Yeah, well, there's way, way too much candy in this

house," Star said, just strongly enough to let him know she wanted to turn down the volume.

"I'll do a little housecleaning," Jimi said, kissing her forehead. "You amuse the band, but remember, you're *my* groupie."

She smiled as he slipped away. He could be such a good guy.

"Okay," Jimi said, waving his arms like a traffic cop. "Mom's home, time to go."

"Who needs a drink?" Star asked, turning back to the more intimate inside crowd in the studio.

Jimi got it down nearer to the originally intended group and their "plus ones," which was still fifty or so, and the odd straggler who'd turn up or regain consciousness in some forgotten room or cranny of the house and wander back into the party. Hank, Theresa, and JC were not around, but Star figured that with Hank's house just down the road they'd moved the little party from her bathroom to the privacy of Hank's bachelor crib.

The band played for a while, then headed out to the pool, where Jimi served dinner off the grill built into the natural rock that they'd used to frame the pool. Dinner wasn't served until around one in the morning, but no one seemed to care.

Star knew she should get to bed for work the next day, but it was turning out to be such a magical night, and they were already home and safe. It was a relief to have a good time when nothing could go wrong.

Eventually, the fact that they were no longer eighteen-year-old rock warriors took its toll, and the professional musicians and their plus ones and twos began to drift away for the evening. As Star and Jimi were closing the gates behind the last of the guests, and Mutley made one last check of the bushes before following them upstairs to his place in the chair at the foot of the bed, the house phone began to ring.

"Who can that be?" Star wondered. It was almost morning.

"I'll go," Jimi said, trotting across the lawn.

Jimi didn't come back out or call her, so she figured that it must have been someone from the party who'd forgotten something, otherwise it was too late for anyone in that hemisphere to be phoning. She had a nice walk around the big yard with Mutley, then headed inside, where she found Jimi, still on the phone, looking grave and writing away.

"What?" Star said, surprised to see that Jimi was still up, let alone still on the phone. "What is it?"

"Hank's in jail."

"What?" Star said, genuinely not comprehending.

Jimi might as well have said "The Martians have taken Washington." It just didn't make sense, didn't fit somehow.

"He was arrested for dealing drugs," Jimi said, holding his hand over the mouthpiece. "I woke up the lawyer and I'm on hold to see what we can do about bail tonight."

"Hank, my brother?" Star asked, her brow knit. "It's a mistake." She slid down the wall and sat on the floor. How was it possible?

Their lawyer arranged for Hank to sit out the night in an office at the police station where he'd been brought after his arrest, then be taken directly to be arraigned, without ever having to actually be in jail.

As it turned out, the arraignment never happened. The lawyer met with Hank in the police chief's office to get an idea what they were up against. Star went along to see if she could talk to her brother and find out what had happened.

The sun was just rising as she and the lawyer were admitted to see Hank in the sterile, no-frills office.

"Hank," she said, throwing her arms wide.

"Star, I'm so glad to see you," he said, falling between her arms, his head on her shoulder. It had been a long time since the old days when he'd come to her frightened by a storm or a bully or one of their parents' fights. They held each other for a bit.

"Are you okay?" she asked intently, holding him at arm's length to look at him and see for herself.

"Yeah, I'm fine," he sighed. "Considering."

"Then what the hell happened?" she demanded, smacking him sharply on the shoulder. "You scared the hell out of me."

"It was an accident," he pleaded.

"An accident?" she asked incredulously. "You were accidentally dealing drugs?"

"I was not dealing drugs," he said indignantly. "JC was dealing drugs. I was just in the car when he ran into the back of the police cruiser."

"He ran into a police car?" Star said, the hint of a smile beginning to crack her stony expression.

Hank nodded.

"With a carload of drugs?"

"Pretty much."

"Well, thank God Theresa wasn't with you," Star said, strangely relieved by the way things were unfolding.

They held each other and laughed.

10

the light

By the time Hank made bail, the press had not only convicted Hank of being a West Coast drug kingpin, despite no charges ever being filed, they'd also "discovered" that Star was a heroin addict. True, she had been more adventurous about "experimenting" since she and Jimi had gotten together. True, some of those experiments were extensive enough to have qualified as FDA studies. But not only was she not a heroin addict, she'd never even tried it.

Star heard the news of her alarming addiction while listening to the radio in her car one morning on the way to work. This curious and unexpected fact about herself came to her with the aid of Andy Callas. Star had tuned him in to let Andy do the talking on the way to the set.

"And did you see this thing about Star Deed?"

"Who?" said Jai, the woman who worked with Andy on the air.

"Star Leigh. Okay, Jai, it's time to let that go. She changed her name, okay?"

"That's just wrong, Andy."

"Hey, I don't make the rules."

"Star has certainly been in the news a lot lately."

"Too bad about her brother's getting arrested and all," Andy said, clearly not aware of the charges having been dropped. "He's a drug dealer, apparently, and now I see in this morning's papers that she's a heroin addict."

"That really is a shame. Do you think that's true?" Jai asked, knowing when to tee her boss up so he could drive it home.

"Yeah, well, I'll tell you," Andy said pensively, "if she is, she's the healthiest-looking heroin addict I have ever seen."

Star turned off the radio.

"Well, what's next?" she said to Mutley as they arrived for another brutal day of running in the sand. "Come on, boy."

She liked being able to take her old pal with her to the set from time to time. She didn't do it every day since he had a yard of his own, but she loved the extra affection and company.

"We heard," said Billy as she followed Mutley into the trailer. "You okay?"

"Glad I look healthy," she moaned, falling into the chair. "When is it ever enough?"

"We figured that you'd be pretty upset. How's Jimi taking it?" Skip asked.

"I don't know if he's heard," Star said. "He doesn't usually listen to Andy."

"It was in the trades and the tabloids too." Skip pointed at the papers on the couch.

"Oh, God," Star whined as she read the headlines. "FORMER ROADIE SUES FOOLS BRIGADE. This is the sue-me state."

"Hello," Billy called, wiggling his fingers in a little wave as he held up his hands. "Skip and I have opted not to sue you in favor of writing a really vicious tell-all book after your career tanks."

"You two," Star said, pinching his cheek affectionately. "You are true Hollywood friends."

"So, you didn't know?" Skip said, whipping up some magic chemicals to tame the roots he'd spotted as Star had first slumped into the chair that morning.

"About this lawsuit?" Star said, pointing at the paper. "First I heard of it."

"Well, then what was it you were talking about?" Skip said, setting the bowl of dangerous chemicals aside and adjusting her posture as he put a plastic cape around her.

"I'm a heroin addict."

"Oh. Yeah, that does sound pretty awful," Skip teased. "So put some down below too. Here's an extra teaspoon to make sure the carpet matches the drapes." He handed her the bowl of bleach.

She was shooting a scene with the show's star, Foster that morning. As head lifeguard, his character frequently offered guidance and sage advice to his little grasshoppers. Despite his serious character, being in a scene with him was a rollercoaster ride, though Star loved him just the same. He'd been the brains behind the show and she looked up to him.

Typically, he'd do his part of the shoot and leave. The person "sharing" the screen with him acted to a piece of tape on a stick at Foster's eye level with someone else reading Foster's dialogue. The only thing more nerve-racking was when Foster actually stayed to do the scene, as Star was experiencing that morning. While he was on the set with her, he was also talking on two cell phones between his lines and during hers, making bets on horse races. It was amazing how he could manage both at once.

The sun went behind a cloud and the director called cut on the scene. It was a big cloud, and Star took the opportunity to call Mutley over and take a little walk on the beach.

She paused to look out over the water. The ocean always made her feel in perspective somehow. It was so vast and so eternal and so unfathomable. Standing at the water's edge, she could see herself the right size. Not bigger-than-life, as on the *Hy Voltz* movie screen, but tiny and powerless in the face of how big life really was.

For the first time in a long time, the two creases disappeared from between her eyes. Her spider sense was tingling and she knew just what to do. The sun came out from behind the cloud and she raced back to the setup to finish the scene.

"Cut. Excellent, Star," Brock said, seeming genuinely surprised. Oftentimes the call was "If it's in focus, print it." But there had been a new life to Star's performance.

"Thanks, Brock, am I done?" she asked genially.

"Check the schedule, but as far as I know," Brock said, giving her a little wave. "Okay, people, we've got two more setups this afternoon. Let's act like we care!" he shouted to the crew, clapping his hands.

"Come on, Mutley," Star said, racing back to the car.

For the first time in a long time she knew just what to do. She wasn't a victim. She had a choice and she was willing to make it.

Star ran past the trailer, waving to Billy and Skip, who were working on their tans on lounge chairs outside. "I'll see you tomorrow," she called, rushing to the car.

"But, Star," Billy called, sitting up. "The suit."

She looked down, realizing she was still wearing the navy blue one-piece she'd made famous. "I'll bring it back tomorrow."

Star raced Mutley back to the car and climbed behind the wheel. She knew just how to handle the new lawsuit as well as their standoff with the press, and couldn't wait to tell Jimi.

The roadie in question had been injured in an accident at one of the stops on the band's last tour. Rather than take care of him, the guys replaced him and didn't help him out with his bills. Ironically, he'd sued only when he saw the announcement of the new concert date, figuring that if the band was getting back together, there would have to be money involved.

By comparison to the rest, it was just a nuisance lawsuit, but it was the straw that broke the camel's back.

"Jimi!" she shouted, running in the front door like George Bailey returning home after waking from his dark vision. Mutley barked joyously as he followed her in. "Jimi, are you home?"

"Out here, babe," he called from the room they called their office, really just part of the laundry room where they kept their files. Jimi was sitting at the desk talking on the phone when she found him, his feet up on the edge of the old metal monstrosity she'd found at a secondhand furniture store and had refurbished.

"Jimi, I know what to do," Star said excitedly. "I figured it all out today."

"I'm on with the lawyer," he said, covering the mouthpiece. "I don't know if you heard, but there's a lawsuit."

"Isn't it great? I know just what to do. Hang up."

"What?" Jimi said, confused by her enthusiasm. He was still in the old mood, the one she knew how to fix. "Can't it wait?"

"Hey," Star said, grabbing the phone. "McBride? It's Star. How are you? . . . Well, you should take a break. Get some lunch. Charge it to us. Take the afternoon off. It's a beautiful day for a walk on the beach. It would be a shame to waste it in Century City. We'll call you later. . . . Great, bye."

She hung up the phone and climbed onto Jimi's lap, straddling him as she planted a big kiss right on him. He responded by wrapping his arms around her.

"I love this solution," he said in a sleepy, deep voice, drunk with his passion.

"No, no." Star sat up. "This isn't it. That's just the kind of Hi-honey-I'm-home kiss you should be getting from me every day. We're newlyweds, for fuck sake."

"We sure are." He nuzzled her, not quite ready to talk.

"Jimi, Jimi." She took his face in her hands. "I know just what to do. I know just how to handle all this."

"Okay, what is it?" he sighed.

"Surrender," Star said with a shrug. "We don't have to fight."

"What are you talking about?"

"I mean it. This roadie who's suing? He's right. You should pay his medical bills. And you can. So settle it. I think we should settle it all."

"What about the rest of it?" he said, sitting up.

"I can't hide and fight anymore." Star threw her arms into the air. "I can't. I'm done. What difference does it make anymore? My life is worth more than this. Our life is worth more than this. I cannot, will not spend it fighting with people I don't even want to talk to. Don't you see? In a hundred years, who'll care?"

"Yeah, I see," Jimi said, a smile spreading across his face. "I do see. You're right." His mood was rising to match hers.

"You know what we should do?" Star said mischievously, taking his hand and rising from her seat on his lap.

"Yes," he said.

11

the bitch is back

The trip to Paris was perfectly timed.
The freedom of surrender had reinvigorated her life with Jimi. He was in love with her and his music, so her life got better. *Hammer Time* continued to dominate the ratings, and *Lifeguards* was the number one syndicated show in the world. Her career was fine.

Hank was working on *Hammer Time,* making work connections and staying away from the other kind. He was even dating Theresa—a little weird, Star thought, but whatever.

As if she needed a prize for having such a great life, Star was being given a humanitarian award for her service in the cause of animal rights through B.A.G.L.E. And the frosting on that cake was that the award was being presented in Paris.

It was the perfect opportunity for a romantic getaway for two. Star had never been, and their schedules allowed for a little time following the ceremony to discover the legendary city of love together.

The sprinkle on the frosting was that Star was to receive the award from rock legend Sir Andrew Manchester, one of her favorite musicians and a longtime supporter of the animal rights cause. It was the first time the award, named after Sir Andrew's late wife, had ever been presented.

The trip even timed out perfectly with Star's production schedule, though to be honest, she had wheedled, begged, pleaded, and bullied anyone who could help create the time for her departure. The big, top-secret, season finale with Sven was up on her return, and Jimi's New York concert was happening almost simultaneously. Star and Jimi were thinking of taking the summer off to be with each other after a pretty rocky first year. But they both hoped that the concert would jump-start Jimi's career, so their summer plans were filed under wait and see.

A few days in Paris at the George V and an award from Drew Manchester at the Tuileries for being kind to animals was the dream weekend getaway for a girl from Arcady Key.

The trip began with an adventure. They left Hank to look after things, and Lito got them to the airport. Because the purpose of the trip was so visible, their departure was far from secret. They were amazed as throngs of screaming fans descended on her and Jimi.

Breathless with fear, they stood frozen as the mob closed in on them.

"Run," Jimi whispered urgently into her ear at the last moment.

Star turned to look at him and caught the spirit of his grin. It wasn't running to get away, it was a game of chase.

She grinned back.

It was on.

They took off running down the long, tiled passageway into the depths of LAX. The mob was surprised at first, and that gave Star and Jimi a bit of a lead, but it wasn't much. Screaming with delight, the dozens who had somehow gotten on the other side of security took off after them. It turned out that many of their pursuers had actually purchased tickets with no intention of flying, just to be in the terminal with Star and Jimi.

They gave their pursuers quite a run for their money, turning over brochure racks and dropping things in their pursuers' path, managing to get just far enough ahead following a sharp turn that they had time out of sight to hide behind an idle ticket desk. The hardest part of not getting caught was not laughing. Eventually, they got to the first-class cabin of their flight and took their seats.

Seated across the aisle from them was Star's rather intimate acquaintance Randy Pizarro. She had not seen him since she'd escaped from his clutches and his bedroom, giving him the slip by hiding in the guest bathroom.

Star laughed at the private joke between them.

The flight to Paris was long and uneventful. They had dinner and a bit too much champagne, then passed out with the help of a little Ambien. They woke up refreshed and completely out of sync with Paris time.

The press and the crowds were there in force for their arrival, but the security was ready for it. The event planners had escorts and a car there to see them smoothly through customs and into the country.

The director of B.A.G.L.E., Mike Dean, met them at the hotel and saw them to their suite, all the while briefing them on their itinerary. Star didn't know him well, but Mike had a mischievous quality that appealed to her. He was tall and wickedly good-looking with a Southern gentleman's charm that Star felt right at home with. Yet she had learned from their few conversations that he was quite the party boy. They quickly discovered that they had everything in common and that both were big punk fans, as well as animal lovers. They didn't get to spend much time together in Paris, but Star decided to change that situation at the earliest opportunity.

There was a lot to do in their short visit, but thankfully she and Jimi had a little time on their own after Mike dropped them off at the Louis Quatorze Suite. It was exquisite and romantic and the two were glad to have some quality time alone.

They made the most of it.

Their clothes were soon strewn from the front door, across the sitting room, past the blazing fireplace, like a path to the bed.

Star knew how sensitive his nipples were and that rubbing his chest and tugging at his nipple rings while she went down on him drove him nuts and pushed him toward the brink. He had to fight his way back, unwilling for it to end too quickly.

Jimi had brought a Chinese basket in his suitcase, a canvas sling that supported one partner at waist level for easy access when you fuck standing up. They made full use of it that afternoon. The mysterious holes in the ceiling of their room left the staff at the grand old hotel wondering.

All too soon, their serenity was shattered by two familiar voices.

"Hi, kids, how's the show going?" Skip called, letting himself and Billy into the main room.

"Cut," Billy called. "That's a wrap."

"Hi, boys," Jimi said, coming into the room in one of the sumptuous white terry robes the hotel supplied. "She'll be right with you, we just got out of the shower."

"Thanks, Jimi," Skip said, setting out his things on the marquetry table covered with inlaid roses. "And, um, your cock is out."

"Oh, sorry." Jimi grabbed his robe and pulled it more tightly together.

Billy grinned. "Don't worry, we're professionals. We've seen more naked people than most doctors."

"I guess that is a hazard of your job," Jimi said sheepishly.

"Our job?" Skip said, putting his hands on his hips as he considered. "I guess we do see a lot of naked people at work, too."

"Now that you mention it," Billy agreed, nodding.

"Don't pick on Jimi," Star said, coming in bundled in a similar robe. "In fact, if there's time, Skip, maybe you can do something fun with his hair while I'm in makeup."

Jimi looked less than thrilled at the prospect.

"Now who's picking on him?" Billy teased.

"She's a remarkable woman of many talents who has worked tirelessly with B.A.G.L.E. and other animal rights groups to raise public awareness not only of problems but of solutions," Sir Andrew said from the microphone in front of a crowd of people Star had only imagined seeing in person. And now she was not only one of them, but they were there to honor her.

"But don't take my word for it," he went on with the introduction. "I could hardly describe it all. We have a most revealing video. Not that kind of video," he said, riding over the gentle laughter as Star and Jimi shared a nervous glance.

As Star watched along with everyone else, tears came into her eyes. She was proud of herself for making it there. It all seemed worth it somehow. She could see how much her crazy life had meant in the fight for a cause that she'd been rolling pennies for since her childhood.

The applause and the chunk of crystal etched with her name that Drew handed her paled next to the look of pride on Jimi's face as he rose to applaud her.

"I feel like I'm accepting this award on behalf of the people who do the real work," Star said, trying not to cry. "If what I do can help draw attention to their work, then I guess I've helped a little. There's a lot more to be done and we all have to get involved. But tonight, I pay tribute to all those people around the world who are truly making a difference. Thank you."

It was simple and eloquent and very Star. Never one to take all the glory nor to neglect to give credit where it was due, her words went out around the world, beating her home—though not by as much as she'd originally planned.

Hank had gone out to Star and Jimi's house to watch them on the big screen, and his discoveries there would ultimately bring her Paris trip to an early conclusion and change their lives forever.

After the event, Star and Jimi were piled into a car with Mike, Sir Andrew, and his wife, Blanche, for a short ride to a small after party in Star's honor.

She could not have been more thrilled. She had thought that she was only going to get to see Drew onstage when he gave her the award, but they had actually spent some time together and even got to meet his activist wife, Blanche, whose cruelty-free fashion line Star was wearing that evening. Jimi's first opportunity to meet the rock legend and his wife was in the car, where Mike made introductions.

After the banquet in her honor, they returned to the hotel, where Star picked up a message from Hank.

Jimi hit the bed as soon as they got back and left Star dialing the phone. He found her, hours later, still in the gown she'd been in the night before, unable to speak or stop crying.

Jimi had brought along some speed to get them past the jet lag, and they'd gotten pretty motivated before the festivities. To avoid any potentially embarrassing questions, instead of calling a doctor in a strange country, he called Skip and Billy, who were staying in somewhat less grand quarters down the hall.

"Star, darling," Billy said, kneeling beside her. She only clutched him and sobbed harder in reply.

"Did anything happen tonight that might have upset her?" Skip asked, trying to get some sense of the situation. She had seemed almost joyful only a few hours earlier when they were getting her ready.

"Not really," Jimi said, baffled by the outburst.

The two looked on helplessly as Billy held her in his arms and rocked her gently for a bit, until she fell asleep.

"Here," he whispered to Jimi and Skip. "Help me get her to bed. Maybe if she gets some sleep . . ."

When Jimi lifted her, Billy discovered the note on the tearstained carpet where she'd lain.

"Oh, God," he said softly as he read. "I think I know what's wrong."

"What is it?" Skip asked, looking back over.

"It's a message from Hank."

" 'My North, my South, my East and West,' " Star read to the small group gathered in rows of gold cane catering chairs in the big living room at Jimiville. " 'My working week and my Sunday rest. My noon, my midnight, my talk, my song; I thought that love would last forever: I was wrong.' "

Jimi stood sullenly in the back of the room, arms folded as she read the words from a small book of W. H. Auden.

" 'The stars are not wanted now: put out every one.' " She continued reaching out to touch the simple stone urn, glinting in the afternoon sun. " 'Pack up the moon and dismantle the sun; pour away the ocean and sweep up the wood. For nothing now can ever come to any good.' " She concluded her reading and collapsed into tears once again. She had read the same verse at her mother's funeral only weeks before.

Theresa took her hand and helped her to a chair.

Jimi went outside; he couldn't stand it any longer. He bummed a smoke from someone's driver.

Star had been in tears pretty much since he'd found her in their hotel room in Paris. They'd left early, cutting their trip short and returning home to make arrangements. But other than planning for that afternoon, Star had completely withdrawn. She would not eat, she couldn't sleep, save for the few moments when exhaustion overcame her and she dozed, only to wake up screaming.

Jimi had tried to comfort her, but she continued to push him away. He even sheltered her, not telling her about the strange and unnerving phone call from *Scum* magazine offering to buy their sex videos which he knew were still locked away in the safe.

He stomped out the cigarette, and as he returned, saw that the gathering was getting ready to make a move. Star clutched the urn to her breast as the somber little party made their way out to the cars. Jimi fell in behind, riding in silence with Star, the only sound the sobs that accompanied her periodic tears.

They arrived at the marina and boarded the chartered yacht that would take them up the coast to their final destination. Food and drink were served in the main cabin of the luxury cruiser, but Star stood alone at the prow of the ship, caressing the urn as if the act could bring her closer. Jimi fought to contain his anger over the whole farcical afternoon. In a way, he was glad Star did not want him now, because he was too angry with her, with her abandonment, to allow her her grief.

They sailed up the coast for a while, viewing the city from a rarely seen perspective. Despite having one of the busiest harbors in the world, Los Angeles has no real reputation as a seaport and is rarely depicted that way. Whereas New York is always shown from across the river or harbor or from the Atlantic, Los Angeles is almost never shown from the water. It made for an unfamiliar experience for those aboard. Things looked oddly familiar, but they could just as easily have been sailing past a foreign city.

Eventually, the boat pulled even with their house and the captain killed the engines. Star rose and walked to the rail, her black dress billowing in the stiff breeze. She upended the urn and allowed the wind to take the ashes and spread them over the water.

"Good-bye, old friend," Star said softly as she watched the ashes disappear. "You always did want to swim out here; I thought you might like to see it now."

She dropped the urn and sank to her knees, holding on to the railing to keep from falling overboard herself.

Theresa rushed forward to help her. "There, there," she said, stroking Star's hair back out of her face. "It's over now, time to go home."

"It won't be home without Mutley," Star said, dissolving into tears once again.

The guests paid their respects at the slip.

Hank took Theresa to his place while Jimi and Star returned home alone together for the first time since Paris. They rode in silence for a bit. He sighed deeply, unable to think of anything to do or say.

"Don't you care that Mutley is dead?" Her accusation broke the icy silence between them.

"Don't you care that I'm alive?"

"What does this have to do with you?" Star asked bitterly.

"Exactly," he snapped. "You have shut me out. You care more about that damn dog than you do about me."

"Is that all you can think about?" Star's tears came again as she struggled not to let go.

"Stop being such a soap opera queen," he sighed, looking out the window.

"Don't you get it?" she demanded, pounding his shoulder as the tears threatened to take her voice. "He was all alone. I left him here all by himself and he died alone. It's my fault he's dead."

"What are you talking about?"

"I feel like there is a curse on us," Star said, nearly hysterical. "Ever since Cabo. It's like fate wants to punish us for enjoying our lives after doing such horrible things. I just wanted to have a little fun, and first Mom and now Mutley is dead."

She cried all the way back to the house, into bed, and off to sleep that night.

When she finally woke up, alone in their room, she looked to the chair where Mutley used to sleep in the hope that it had only been a bad dream. She arose, opened the curtains, and sat in Mutley's chair, staring out to sea as he had so often. She gazed toward the spot where she'd sprinkled his ashes. And that's where Jimi found her when he came home that afternoon.

"Okay," he said. "That's it. You're coming with me."

"I don't feel like it."

"Star, break's over. You've got to get back to the set in two days, and I'm leaving for New York in the morning. Life's in session. Put on a sweatshirt and some jeans or something, but I need for you to come with me."

They regarded each other a moment.

She got up listlessly, went into the dressing room, and found some sweats. "Okay," she said, emerging.

She followed him wordlessly downstairs and got in the car beside him without questioning where they were going.

The weather was beginning to warm up as spring took hold, and she looked out the window and watched the wild-flowers on the banks alongside PCH blur past. After about a half hour's drive, Jimi pulled into the lot by the offices of Mutley's vet.

"Why are we here?" Star asked.

"For the truth." Jimi got out and went around to open Star's door for her. Reluctantly, she took his hand and followed him across the cracked asphalt of the lot.

They went inside and Jimi let the receptionist know they had arrived for their appointment. Star took a seat and looked around at the lobby, filled with pets and their owners. Bandages, the humiliating "Elizabethan" plastic collars, and worried faces filled the room. Star thought that she might have to leave. Her feelings were just too strong.

"Jimi?" the doctor said from the doorway. "Star, good to see you. Come on back."

"What are we doing here?" Star asked Jimi angrily once they were in the little hallway that led from the lobby to the examination rooms. The sounds of dogs yapping and the occasional wail of a cat brought the space alive with pain.

Jimi didn't answer. He took her hand and led her along as they followed the doctor into his office at the end of the hall. The small, warm space was filled with pictures of the doctor, from his youth to the present day, each with him in the company of a series of Weimaraners. Ribbons and diplomas told the story of a love affair that had become a career for the sprightly, curly-haired little man before them.

"Doc, tell Star what you told me," Jimi said.

"It was a heart attack, Star," the doctor said. "And judging from the way that Hank found Mutley, he was asleep when it happened. It was massive and almost instantaneous. He never even woke up. We should all die such a peaceful death."

"But if I'd been there," Star said, crying angrily, "I could have done something. I could have helped him. He wouldn't have been alone."

"No, Star," the doctor said, comforting her. "There was nothing you could have done. If you'd been there, you probably wouldn't even have known. He lay down to go to sleep and never got up again. He was an old dog and it was his time. And you and I have no say in such things. It's as much a part of life as birth."

Her tears stopped after a few minutes.

She looked into the doctor's eyes and around the room at the pictures of the succession of Weimaraners that had filled the doctor's life. She realized how many times he must have had to say good-bye.

She looked at Jimi. He gave her a nod. It wasn't what she'd wanted, but it was what he could give her. It might even have been what she needed. She didn't feel great, but she did see that feeling responsible wasn't loving to Mutley anymore than she already did.

"Time to go on," she said, rising and pushing past him. She took the doctor's hand as they left. "Thanks."

"Do what I do," he said with a sad smile. "Take some time and then get another one. There's a puppy out there that needs to love you just as much as Mutley did."

She smiled at the idea.

Jimi started the car and they drove for a bit in silence.

"Thank you," she said, patting the back of his hand as it rested on the gearshift.

His lips disappeared in a tight smile. It was all he had for her, whether or not it was enough.

12

lovely day

It was one of those perfect L.A. mornings.

The cool breeze blew in early off the Pacific and the clouds dissolved into a clear blue springtime sky. The light was inspiring and the view clear and crisp, as if the whole city had suddenly snapped into focus.

They had awakened from a night of lovemaking and felt as clear and focused as the morning outside their widow. Jimi made them an extraspecial "breakfast," as they would be separated for the first time since that night in Cabo. He was off to New York for the concert and she would join him after she wrapped shooting on *Lifeguards*.

It was a fresh new start, Star thought to herself as she showered and got ready to go to the set. Her mom's last words came back to her once again. "Remember, it's your choice who you are."

Jimi was packing, getting ready for his trip when she came out of the bathroom.

"Jimi," she said, coming up behind him and hugging him from the back. "I was saving it as a surprise, but I can't wait. There's something I want to tell you."

"What is it, babe?" he said, turning to take her in his arms.

The doorbell rang.

"Who is that?" Jimi said. "The car's not supposed to be here for another hour."

"Don't go," Star said, her spider sense on full alert.

"Who is it?" Star whispered as Jimi tried to peer around the edge of the curtains in one of the front bedrooms.

"It's the police," Jimi said, drawing back suddenly from the window.

"Maybe it's nothing," Star suggested as the two rushed to the back of the house.

"There's four at the door and the street out front looks like the parking lot at the sheriff's station." He looked out back and saw the uniformed officers encircling the house.

"How did they get in?" Star said, wondering that the police were inside the gates. "No one has the code but you and me and . . ."

"Hank."

"Not my own brother," Star said, shaking her head in disbelief.

"Did you give them the code?"

She shook her head.

"Well neither did I," he said.

"What are we going to do?" Star said, as the tension of the past months built to the breaking point.

"Come with me," he said, taking her hand.

The officer rang the bell for a third time, but still no answer.

"Maybe they're still asleep," his partner said, standing back from the door, his gun drawn.

"What's happening?" the captain's voice crackled through the officer's walkie-talkie.

"No answer," the officer replied. "Maybe they're still asleep. The brother said they were partiers. What's the next step?"

Before the captain had a chance to answer, the black Ferrari burst through the garage door, the wood panels exploding into splinters as the high-performance projectile rocketed down the drive, through the open gate, and down the street before any of the police on the scene had a chance to draw their service revolvers.

"Woo-hoo," Star screamed as they tore up the canyon road, the police nowhere in sight. "Let's go again."

Jimi laughed in spite of the tension. He knew she was trying to cheer him up.

"Whatever happens, babe, it's been the best ride of my life," he said, taking her hand.

She kissed his knuckles.

"Where to?" he asked her as they rocketed toward Mulholland Drive, the legendary road that snaked along the ridge of the mountains that formed the northern border of the Los Angeles basin.

"Mexico," she said with a shrug. "And then, who knows?"

"You got it," he said, passing a car and nearly running an oncoming truck off a cliff as he continued to pick up speed.

Both were unaware that overhead the police they thought they'd left behind had taken to the air to keep them in sight. Unfortunately, the police weren't the only ones who'd taken up the chase.

"And this just in," Kurt Blanche said, reaching up to touch his earpiece in disbelief. "Police are involved in a high-speed chase in the canyon roads up from Malibu. And . . . are we sure?" he said, looking to the booth for further confirmation as L.A. was waking up to his morning news break-in on the network's morning talk show. "Okay, we have confirmation, the fugitives being pursued are Star Wood Leigh and Jimi Deed, though it's unclear yet why the police want them. We'll keep you posted as the story develops.

By the time Kurt had finished the weather, he was co-anchoring the national news with New York. News helicopters had joined the chase along with those from the L.A.P.D. and Sheriff's Department.

Dozens of radio cars, police helicopters, as well as at least one chopper for each of the networks, had taken up the high-speed pursuit. Morning traffic reports took up the story and thousands, bound for work, called in sick from their cars and headed in the direction of the chase. Traffic arteries in and around the beach began to shut down as the curious poured into the area to get a closer look.

Across the country, work came to a standstill as people clustered in front of any available television set to see what would happen next. In fact, most everyone in the country knew about the chase before Star and Jimi did.

"So, do you think we should take the 405?" Jimi asked, running the light and making the turn onto Mulholland at full speed as cars spun out of control to avoid hitting them. "Traffic may not be as bad southbound."

"I don't know," Star said, trying to find something to listen to on the disc changer. "The 405 is always a nightmare."

Bill Withers's "Lovely Day" came out of nowhere and she had to laugh at the irony. In so many ways, it really was a lovely day.

"What is this doing on here?" she giggled.

"I like all kinds of music," Jimi said, reaching over to try to change the disc. He hit the wrong button, and the radio came on instead.

"The occupants of the car appear to be Star Wood Leigh and husband, Jimi Deed," the announcer was saying.

"Fuck you, dude, her fucking last name is Deed!" Jimi shouted, taking up the gun in his lap and firing a shot at the radio but only blowing off the glove compartment door.

"Jimi, be careful with that," Star said, turning up the volume for details.

"Police are closing in on the couple as they make their way

toward the 405 on Mulholland Drive. Motorists are asked to avoid the area, as they are believed to be armed and dangerous."

Jimi turned the wheel and spun the car, dangerously close to flipping it as he reversed course at such high speed and almost immediately rode head-on into a wall of police cars coming straight for them.

"Jimi, there's something I should tell you!" Star screamed when it looked as though they were about to be plastered across the grille of an oncoming prowl car.

But at the last second, he turned onto a small paved road that swept them rapidly up into the hills above and momentarily away from their pursuers.

"Hang on a second, babe," he said, maneuvering the car into the hills without losing speed.

"Okay," she said, not wanting to distract him as they narrowly escaped death on each turn.

"Evidence has been uncovered linking the couple to the deaths of a series of photographers known in the entertainment business as paparazzi," Kurt said earnestly to his viewers as voice-over to the airborne cameras following Star and Jimi's progress into the hills. "The deaths in this country, Mexico, and possibly Paris had previously been thought to be unrelated, but . . ."

"Hold on, Kurt," Cathy, the New York anchor, broke in. "I'm getting word that we have just acquired exclusive video that links the couple to the crimes. So we're going to cut away to that for a moment and then we'll come back to our live coverage of the Star chase."

The chase squeezed into the corner of the frame as the

scene from the balcony at the El Presidente suite in Cabo San Lucas filled the screen.

"On three? One, two, three."

Their nudity had been digitally masked but the murder was shown on national television. Cathy was mistaken about one thing, the footage was far from exclusive. Hank and Theresa had dubbed off as many copies as they could that night, and while he was working with the police, she had been putting together their retirement fund, selling copies to every network and news outlet in the world.

"I can't believe that," Star said, staring at the radio as they listened for the third time to the photographer's screams as he plunged from their balcony. "How did they get the video? The only person who had the combination for the safe besides you and me was . . ."

"Hank," Jimi snarled, his knuckles turning white as he clutched the steering wheel.

"Well, to be fair, Theresa knows too," Star said. "But then she's dating . . ."

"Hank," Jimi said. "The rat fuck sold us out."

"You don't know that," Star said, trying vainly to defend her beloved brother.

"We take you live to a press conference with Star Wood Leigh's brother, Hank Leigh, as he reveals his tormented decision to turn in his own sister when he discovered evidence of her despicable crimes."

"For the last time her last fucking name is Deed," Jimi said, succeeding in blowing the radio out of the dashboard with his Mauser Hsc.

"Look out!" Star screamed as she saw the metal barrier closing fast in front of the car.

Jimi braked too late.

As the world watched in horror, the little black sports coupe smashed through the barrier, hit the dirt road at the entrance to the small hilltop park, and disappeared into a cloud of dust.

For minutes, as newscasters the world over speculated, the fate of the two was not known as everyone waited for the dust to clear.

"According to park rangers there is a massive drop just a matter of yards from where the car broke through the barrier," Kurt was explaining for the cameras. "Unless they were able to stop in time, they could easily have plunged to their deaths over the cliff, ironically, just like the man believed to be their first victim. We have computer simulations of what that plunge might have looked like."

Hank was annoyed that their deaths had cut his news conference short, but the three movie offers he'd already had that morning went a long way toward helping him get over it. He still could not quite believe the strange series of events that had begun while he was sneaking a peek at the amateur home videos only the night before and landing him on the world stage before lunchtime.

L.A. was a long way from Arcady Key.

"Hello? Andy?"

"Star? Is that you?" Andy Callas said by way of welcome to his on-air guest as Star's voice crackled onto the airwaves of America's most listened to morning radio program. Always at the top of the charts, Andy's show went off the scale when every network and news service around the world went live with his broadcast so that Star spoke to the entire world at once from her cell phone as she and Jimi sat in Topanga State Park waiting for the dust to settle.

"Hi, Andy," Star said, her girlish voice strangely at odds with what the world had just discovered about her only moments before.

"Star, is there anything you'd like to say?"

"Yes," Star said, softly. "I just want to say first that those videotapes were our private property and they were stolen from our home. And secondly, that man broke into our hotel room and photographed us making love on our honeymoon. So, whatever action we took was in self-defense."

"He looked pretty defenseless hanging from that balcony," Andy said in his typical cut-to-the-bone style.

"That's how he broke into our room in the first place," Star said. "It's dangerous hanging from the sides of buildings."

"Anything you want to say to your fans?" Andy asked as he could see on the monitors that the dust was clearing and an army of police cars were closing on them.

"Yeah," Star sighed. "First, thank you for you support. And second, leave us alone."

"Thanks Star, for being on the show today," Andy said. "I hope we'll get the chance to talk to each other again."

"Yeah, me too, Andy," Star said. "Anything you want to say, Jimi?"

"Everyone sucks but us," Jimi's voice, cracking with laughter, came in from the background.

"I love you, babe," Jimi said, taking her hand and kissing it. "It's been the best with you, every, every minute."

"I love you, babe," Star said, kissing his hand, his chest, his neck, and then finding his mouth for a passionate moment, lost in each other once again.

"Jimi," Star said, her eyes brimming with tears. "I have to tell you something."

"No more words, babe," Jimi said, touching her lips to silence her. "No apologies. We've lived our lives full speed and that's how we'll go out."

Jimi stomped the accelerator and, as the world—which had just heard the declarations live via Star's still open cell phone call to Andy Callas—watched in horror, the Testarossa's tires spun in the dust and the car reached nearly 100 m.p.h. as they hurtled toward the cliff that they had chosen as their launching pad.

Unlike the rest of the world, what Jimi and Star could not see was the line of police cars rushing up to cut them off, robbing them of their dramatic final moment and their freedom to choose their own fate.

Jimi spun the car away from the intervening police cruisers to avoid a collision. Chaos ensued. Clouds of dust made it hard to see. Shots were fired, but it was unclear by whom. Star and Jimi leaped from the car to make a run for each other for one final embrace before the officers tore them apart.

"Star, Star!" Jimi screamed straining against the hands of half a dozen officers to get to her as she struggled to reach him.

"Jimi," Star shouted. "I love you, babe."

"I love you, babe."

The police began to jerk her around roughly in an effort to get cuffs on her, knocking her down briefly and then yanking her to her feet again. "Be careful," she screamed. "I'm pregnant."

"What?" Jimi says, going rigid for a moment and then turning into a wild man to try to get to her.

"I'm pregnant," she said tenderly as she was cuffed and led away.

"No!" Jimi screamed, losing control. As the adrenaline kicked in, his strength became almost superhuman, and he began tossing police officers aside like rag dolls. The officers responded in kind and began clubbing Jimi into submission, tackling him to the ground as Star watched in horror.

Despite the beating he was taking, Jimi would not give up his struggle to be at her side and broke free, charging toward Star and the officers surrounding her.

"Let her go!" he screamed, pulling the Mauser from his belt as he charged. "I love you, Star."

Armed and dangerous, the officers opened fire on Jimi.

"I love you, Jimi," Star screamed hysterically as a hail of bullets brought him down before her eyes. Hands restrained her as she tried to get to him when he fell. And a hand on her head as she was forced into the car and driven away. Star clutched her stomach to embrace and protect all that she had left of the man she loved.

"I love you, Jimi," she whispered. "I'll always love you."